'Will you he

Sam froze in dis

Had she really
had sounded like
dreams—beautiful Titian-haired Kirstin
Whittaker asking him to make her pregnant.

'Would I…what?' he croaked huskily, and had
to clear his throat.

It sounded as if he'd swallowed his tongue,
but at least that was better than tripping over it
while his imagination ran riot. While he knew
from intermittent gossip around the
department that she lived alone, that didn't
mean there wasn't a man in her life. There
was no excuse for leaping to the conclusion
that she was asking him to give her a baby.
His body was certainly ready, willing and able
but that *couldn't* be what she wanted.

Or could it?

Josie Metcalfe lives in Cornwall now, with her long-suffering husband, four children and two horses, but, as an army brat frequently on the move, books became the only friends who came with her wherever she went. Now that she writes them herself she is making new friends, and hates saying goodbye at the end of a book—but there are always more characters in her head clamouring for attention until she can't wait to tell their stories.

Recent titles by the same author:

ONE AND ONLY
TWO'S COMPANY

THREE LITTLE WORDS

BY
JOSIE METCALFE

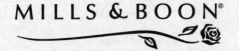

MILLS & BOON®

*First published in Great Britain 2000
Harlequin Mills & Boon Limited,
Eton House, 18-24 Paradise Road, Richmond, Surrey TW9 1SR*

© Josie Metcalfe 2000

ISBN 0 263 82281 8

*Set in Times Roman 10½ on 12 pt.
03-0101-47911*

*Printed and bound in Spain
by Litografia Rosés, S.A., Barcelona*

CHAPTER ONE

'ISN'T he beautiful?' exclaimed Hannah Klein as she cradled her new son in her arms. 'He's still too sleepy to want a feed but I can't resist cuddling him.'

Kirstin looked at the tiny part of the infant visible over the edge of a pristine white blanket and agreed with a smile. No way would she have described the head, still showing the effects of the ventouse delivery, as beautiful but, then, she wasn't the child's mother.

Anyway, the effects were short-lived, and once the swelling and discoloration subsided he would probably look every bit as lovely as every other newborn.

'How are you feeling now?' she prompted, a quick glance at the chart showing that, with the exception of a slightly raised temperature, all the post-delivery observations were normal. There were no particular problems prompting her visit, except that she always wanted to make one last personal check on the patients she'd attended during her shift before she went off duty.

It was a trait she shared with Sam Dysart, the consultant in charge of St Augustine's Obs and Gyn department and her mentor. Even though he'd earned the right to guard his off-duty hours, he'd never been known for hurrying away from his responsibilities either, and she couldn't be happier, working in the same department.

Mrs Klein's delivery was a case in point.

Sam had been on the point of going home when the midwife had reported to Kirstin that the baby's heart rate had started dipping below acceptable levels. He had still been there, hovering around the delivery room, when the situation had rapidly worsened, but by then the delivery had passed the point of no return.

It would have been very easy for him to have stepped in to take over the management of the case but he hadn't interfered, having quietly stayed out of the way in the background.

She'd known he'd been there, of course. It was almost as if she'd developed antennae tuned to his frequency to let her know when he was anywhere within half a mile.

As it was, with her concentration firmly fixed on positioning the ventouse cap exactly right over the baby's head and applying just the right amount of suction, she'd still been conscious of the fact that his dark brown eyes had been watching her every move. It had been a curiously comforting feeling to know that he'd only been there to support her and not with any critical intention of waiting to pounce on errors.

Her relief and pleasure at being able to lay a loudly wailing baby in Hannah Klein's arms had been matched by the smile she'd received from the other side of the room.

'You mean, how am I feeling *apart* from feeling as if I just gave birth to an extremely large cannon-ball?' Hannah Klein groaned, dragging Kirstin's thoughts back to the present. 'Actually, I think I'm feeling too euphoric that he's really here and he's safe to pay too much attention to any aches and pains. He's worth every bit of it.'

'Even the stitches?' Kirstin prompted, tongue-in-cheek.

'Well, maybe not,' her patient admitted wryly. 'It's not too bad if I stay still, but if I try to move...or go to the bathroom...'

'Pinch a bit?' Kirstin frowned. Once she'd made the decision that a ventouse delivery had probably been the only way to rescue the situation, the urgency had required a slightly larger than usual episiotomy. She was sure she hadn't put the stitches in too tightly when she'd tidied everything up, but if the tissues had swollen more than expected...

'Pinching? That's a nice way of putting it,' she said with a chuckle, closely followed by a wince. 'Actually, I don't think they're as bad as last time, when the baby didn't have to be dragged out that way, but all I can say is I'll be glad when they can be taken out.'

'If you're not happy, make certain someone calls me,' Kirstin instructed with a surreptitious glance at her watch. It wasn't long before the end of her shift, and there was no one in active labour at the moment—not that the situation couldn't change without a moment's warning.

Still, the staff had her pager number, as well as that of her mobile phone, if necessary. They knew she didn't live very far away, and even on foot she could be here pretty quickly.

'As you've already got one little one at home, you've opted to stay here for just forty-eight hours. We want to make certain we don't send you home with any problems, especially ones that we could easily have sorted out on the ward. You'll have enough on your hands, trying to deal with two little ones, without problems with your stitches.'

With a last admiring look at the peacefully sleeping bundle, she made her farewells.

'Psst! Kirstin!' came a voice from the doorway as she made her way towards it, but the only thing visible was a beckoning hand.

'Who…? Naomi!' she exclaimed with a delighted grin as they fell into step. Ever since they'd met twelve years ago as rebellious misfits in the foster-care system, they'd developed a friendship closer than that of most sisters. 'What's the matter? Why all the cloak-and-dagger routine?'

'Have you got a minute?' Naomi had a wide smile on her face but, then, ever since she and Adam Forrester had married, the pair of them seemed to be going around with smiles on their faces all the time. It was almost enough to make Kirstin feel thoroughly left out, especially when Cassie, the third member of their surrogate sisterhood, and her husband Luke joined them for a meal.

'I've got several minutes, in fact,' she said, beckoning Naomi towards the small staffroom a little further along the corridor. 'I'll even make you a big mug of real coffee.'

'Thanks, Kirstin, but, no, thanks,' Naomi said hurriedly, grabbing her arm. 'Actually, that's why I wanted to see you. To tell you before the grapevine got hold of the news.'

'Tell me what?' Kirstin frowned and leaned back against the work surface, her hands braced on the edge at either hip. 'What news?'

'That you won't have to make me any coffee for

the next seven months or so,' her friend said, clearly excited by the idea. 'Oh, Kirstin, I'm so happy.'

'No coffee? Why? Are you and Adam moving to another hospital or something? Don't tell me the two of you signed up for this international exchange thing?'

Several colleagues from different departments in the hospital had recently returned from various parts of the globe where they'd spent time walking in the shoes of their opposite numbers. It was amazing just how much it helped to raise standards in each participating hospital when they compared their relative criteria of 'best practice'.

The trouble was, there had been so many changes over the last few weeks. Up until then, with all three of them working in their dream jobs at St Augustine's, they'd always managed to get together at intervals, even if only for a hasty cup of coffee. Since both of Kirstin's friends had married, things had changed, and if Naomi was going to be moving away, even for a short while...

'We're not going anywhere!' Naomi exclaimed impatiently. 'It's not like you to be so slow, especially since you work in Obstetrics and Gynaecology. I'm pregnant, Kirstin! Adam and I are going to have a baby! Isn't it fantastic?'

'Fantastic!' Kirstin echoed weakly as she tightened her fingers around the edge of the work surface. She was stunned and shamed by the unexpected twist of jealousy that gripped her heart, especially as marriage and motherhood had never figured in her own dreams.

'I knew you'd be pleased for us,' Naomi bubbled, apparently oblivious to her friend's shocked reaction. She was almost bouncing with excitement. 'It must have happened almost straight away, on our honey-moon.'

'Honeymoon?' Kirstin teased, dragging herself to-gether with a monumental effort. 'The two of you only had a long weekend!'

'Well, we worked very hard at it,' Naomi said out-rageously.

'Obviously.' Kirstin was still shaken by her reac-tion to her friend's news but at least it didn't seem to be obvious. She would hate for Naomi to think she wasn't delighted for her, especially when it was prob-ably no more than a passing fit of petty resentment.

It had been bad enough when first Cassie and then Naomi had married so quickly. After all the years the three of them had spent together, supporting and en-couraging each other, it still felt almost as if the two of them had abandoned her.

Still, she'd been able to rationalise that. After all, she was the only one of the three who had always been adamant that she didn't want to marry, didn't want to leave herself open to the pain of abandon-ment.

She couldn't help the sad realisation that, now Naomi was pregnant, motherhood would be another link that the two of them would share, even though Jenny was really Cassie's child by adoption.

It was also another way that the two of them—four, if she counted Luke and Adam—were excluding her from their charmed circle.

'How about some tea, instead?' she asked brightly as she reached across to switch on the kettle, hoping her less than cheerful thoughts hadn't been visible on her face. The last thing she wanted was to take the shine off Naomi's happiness.

'As long as you don't make it too strong or put too much milk in it,' Naomi warned. 'I'm already far too familiar with the pattern of the tiles around my toilet.'

'Being sick already?' This was more familiar territory for Kirstin. This could be a conversation with any of her expectant mums at the antenatal clinic.

'Not much, so far. But I feel so ghastly first thing in the morning that I almost daren't leave the loo just in case I *do* throw up!'

'And if you obey the law of averages, you've still got another month or so to go before you start feeling better,' Kirstin warned.

'I really didn't need you to remind me about that,' Naomi grumbled, her hand hovering longingly over a chocolate biscuit for a moment before she settled for a plain digestive instead. 'And don't you dare mention stretch marks and swollen ankles and all the other depressing bits I've got to look forward to. All I want to do at the moment is bask in the wonder of it all.'

'The wonder of *what*?' came a third voice as Cassie walked into the little staffroom. 'I got Naomi's message to come up here, so what's up?'

'You mean, apart from everything I swallow?' Naomi grumbled, but she couldn't help the huge grin that belied her complaint.

Kirstin felt guilty all over again when she witnessed Cassie's genuine delight at their friend's news.

'Have you told Dot yet?' Cassie demanded, bringing a genuine smile to Kirstin's face at last.

They all knew how much their foster-mother had always loved babies. She and Arthur had taken care of dozens of them before cancer had come between them. 'What did she say? I bet she's over the moon at the prospect of another grandchild.'

'I haven't told her yet. Adam and I are going over to see her this evening,' Naomi explained happily. 'We decided we'd like to tell her in person rather than over the phone, but I couldn't wait to tell the two of you first.'

'What's the betting she'll have all the usual goodies already on hand?' Cassie said. 'I wouldn't be surprised if she's already started knitting. She has the most amazing intuition as far as the three of us are concerned.'

'She'd say it was from years of needing eyes in the back of her head,' Kirstin said wryly. 'She hardly knew what we were going to get up to next when we first arrived.'

'Ah, but we did eventually grow up and gain a bit of common sense,' Naomi pointed out, then turned to Cassie. 'It must have been like old times for her when you and Luke pulled that stunt, pretending to fall in love and get married when he was just trying to get custody of Jenny.'

'She saw through that pretty quickly,' Cassie said with a wry grin. 'Anyway, I *was* in love with him, right from the start. And now that we've got full custody of Jenny…'

There was no doubting that the two of them were in love *now*, Kirstin thought with another twinge of something suspiciously green-eyed. Seeing how happy her two friends were, it was almost enough to make her rethink her long-held beliefs.

Almost, but not enough, she rationalised when she had some space to herself a little later.

Her meeting with her two friends had been rudely interrupted by the all-too-familiar sound of her pager and she'd been almost relieved that it had been a call from Accident and Emergency.

The young couple waiting for her looked almost grey with worry.

'Mr and Mrs Leask, my name is Dr Kirstin Whittaker,' she began, but didn't manage to get any further.

'She's bleeding, Doctor,' the muscular young man said, the words almost an accusation.

'Am I losing the baby?' his slender partner pleaded, clearly distraught.

'How long have you been pregnant?' Kirstin asked. The details were on the case notes, but asking the couple to concentrate on answering questions was a good enough way to avert hysteria until she had something to tell them.

'Just ten weeks,' he said. 'She only had a scan a couple of days ago and they said everything was fine then.'

'Well, we'll do another scan in a few minutes,' Kirstin promised, needing nothing more than a swift glance in the direction of the accompanying staff nurse for her to hurry out of the cubicle to arrange it. 'But in the meantime I need to ask a few more questions. Mrs Leask, have you had any pain? Or even a series of pains coming in waves?'

'No. Nothing like that,' she said with pathetic eagerness. 'Is that a good thing?'

'It can be,' Kirstin confirmed cautiously. 'And can you think of anything that's happened to you in the last few hours that might have caused a problem? Have you had any problems with your waterworks? Any discomfort or signs of infection? How about accidents? Any falls?' Unfortunately, there were so many possible causes that it was almost impossible to rule them all out. Sometimes she wondered how *any* babies made it to full term.

'No. Nothing.' The frightened woman shook her head, her limp blonde hair straggling over the collar of her fleecy jacket. 'I've even had a few days off work while we move into the new flat.'

'You've been moving house?' Alarm signals were beginning to flash. That was one of the most stressful things they could have done even if she hadn't been pregnant. And for the move to take place in the first trimester of a pregnancy...

'We moved today,' she confirmed simply. 'We weren't going far—only moving from an upstairs flat to one on the ground floor in the same building, ready for when the baby arrives—so we've even been able to do it ourselves without paying hundreds of pounds to a removals company.'

'You weren't shifting furniture?' Kirstin hoped she was keeping the horror out of her voice. It wouldn't be the first time that a mum-to-be had taken on an enormous task in preparation for her baby's arrival, only to lose the baby because the stresses on her body were too great.

'Of course not,' the husband retorted swiftly, apparently insulted that Kirstin thought he would have let his wife do something so stupid. 'A gang of my mates from work helped me to do all the heavy stuff this morning, in return for a blow-out on pizza and beer at lunchtime.'

'Honestly, Doctor,' her patient said earnestly, 'they would only let me stand there and point to where I wanted things to go. They only left me the bits and pieces to organise. All I had to do was put the pots and pans away in the kitchen, put our clothes in the cupboards and make the bed—oh, and hang the curtains up.'

Kirstin groaned silently at the last item on an already strenuous list but didn't have a chance to say anything as the technician, Trish Atkinson, arrived just then, wheeling in the trolley with the ultrasound machine.

It was only a few minutes before the results were ready but it must have seemed like an aeon or two to the waiting parents-to-be. Their hands were clasped tightly together for mutual support as they gazed with awful fascination at the fuzzy shadows on the screen.

'You saw the first scan just a few days ago, so you'll probably be able to pick out the most important part,' Kirstin began with a silent sigh of relief. 'As you can see, the baby's heart is still beating perfectly normally, so he or she is still very much alive.'

Kirstin was always delighted to be able to give a positive report. It could so easily have been bad news.

'We'll take a urine specimen to check for infection, but I think it's possible that you might have overdone the unpacking and the curtain-hanging. My advice is that you let the man of the house do those jobs for the foreseeable future.'

'So I'm not losing the baby?' Tonya Leask pleaded, obviously desperate to hear it in words of one syllable.

'Not as far as we can see,' Kirstin hedged, wary of promising anything too categorically. 'Unfortunately, your pregnancy is right at the time where a lot of women lose babies spontaneously—without doing any curtain-hanging.'

'When *will* we know for certain, Doctor?' her

stocky partner demanded. 'And is there anything *we* can do to stop her losing it?'

'There's really only one thing you can do to give the baby the best possible chance—make sure Tonya rests a lot over the next few days. Only essential trips such as to the toilet. Feet up. No housework. No cooking. And absolutely no shopping,' she added with a quick grin in his direction.

His expression lightened marginally and he pretended to wipe his forehead in relief that his wife wouldn't be able to go out spending any money.

'And then?' Tonya prompted fearfully, oblivious of the exchange going on around her.

'And then, when you've had several days without any further bleeding, you can start to get back to normal—bearing in mind that hanging curtains is not usually classed as normal for a pregnant woman.'

'*Why* did this have to happen? Is there something wrong with me?' she asked tearfully, still inclined to look on the black side. 'None of my friends have had problems like this.'

'You'd be surprised,' Kirstin said, remembering her own amazement the first time Sam had brought the statistics to her notice. 'The figures can be quite hair-raising. Apparently, something like eighty per cent of fertilised eggs never get as far as being implanted in the womb. If you look at it that way, you're already on the winning end of the numbers game when some people *never* make it.'

Kirstin saw all too many of those desperate souls at St Augustine's fertility clinic. At least they were lucky enough to have been referred to someone as sympathetic and as skilled as Sam Dysart.

Already, in the short time since she'd joined his

team, she had met some who had reached just this stage of a pregnancy over and over again without ever getting any further.

She jotted the obs and gyn unit's direct telephone number on a leaflet full of helpful information and handed it to them.

'If you're still worried, ring that number,' she suggested. 'It goes straight through to the department and there'll be someone on the other end ready to give you advice.'

As she made her farewells, she sent up a silent prayer that this young couple wouldn't need to use the number. It would be nice to think that they would complete the pregnancy without heartbreak.

Back up in Obs and Gyn all was relatively quiet. There was just her and a pile of paperwork that needed finishing before she could go home with a clear conscience.

For a moment her thoughts followed the young couple on their way home, but clearest in her mind was the little scene their emergency had interrupted—the trio's celebration of Naomi's newly announced pregnancy.

Each time Kirstin went over it in her head, it stopped like a freeze-frame in a film when she got to the ecstatic expression on Naomi's face.

'Adam and I are going to have a baby! Isn't it fantastic?'

Each time she replayed it, Kirstin was gripped by the same strange aching hollowness that left her feeling quite sick.

'Problem?' a deep voice asked.

She twisted in her seat and found herself looking up into Sam's familiar face. Dark hair and dark eyes lent an air of intensity to the lean planes, and concern was as clear in his expression as it had been in his tone.

Suddenly, she was gripped with the crazy desire to pour out her thoughts, and before she could control it she heard the first words emerging.

'I was just wondering if I've made the right decisions,' she said, and was aghast to hear the uncertainty in her voice. It made her sound almost weak and indecisive and that was something she could never allow to happen.

'What sort of decisions?' he prompted as he perched one hip on the corner of the desk as if he had all the time in the world to listen. 'A problem with a patient?'

She shook her head and pressed her lips together but that wasn't enough to stop the unstoppable.

'My life,' she said, then gave a nervous chuckle. 'That sounds terribly melodramatic, doesn't it? But...'

She paused, then realised that there was only one way to make sense of the situation—to start at the beginning. 'Cassie, Naomi and I first met when we were fifteen. A social worker sent the three of us to the same foster-home. Have you heard us mention Dot and Arthur?'

'Not only that, but I actually met Dot at Cassie's wedding,' he said with a smile. 'She's an amazing little lady.'

'Well, she might not be very big, but she certainly turned our lives around,' Kirstin said with feeling. It still amazed her sometimes how Dot had tapped into the fact that, in spite of their disastrous childhoods, the three of them had still had dreams.

The dark slash of his raised eyebrow was enough to spur her into an explanation, all discomfort at the unaccustomed openness fading in the face of his obvious interest.

'Twelve years ago, we were a trio of misfits on the fast road to nowhere...until Arthur was diagnosed with cancer. Almost overnight we discovered what was important to us, and that if we really wanted something—if there was a special dream that really mattered—we would have to be prepared to fight and work for it.'

'And what did you decide to fight for?'

Talking about those times usually left Kirstin feeling raw and defensive, but the fugitive gleam of humour in Sam's eyes was like balm to her soul. It was almost as if he really understood what she was talking about...but how could he? A man of his age, with his qualifications, had obviously been on a fast track to success all his life.

Even so, she'd never realised before just how easy it was to talk to him. He didn't stand on his dignity in the least with patients but she'd never thought that she would ever sit here talking to him about her feelings with the same ease as she once had with Cassie and Naomi.

'Ever since I can remember, I've wanted security and independence,' she said quietly, just the sound of the words seeming to wrap around her like a familiar blanket.

'After my parents were gone, I was all alone and there were far too many years when I was moved around at the whim of bureaucracy. Once the three of us had settled in with Dot and Arthur, we decided that the only way to stop it happening again was to refuse, point-blank, to move.'

She had a momentary vision of that harassed social worker's face when the three of them had refused to leave the first place that had ever felt like a real home. The woman had honestly thought that Arthur's illness had been a good reason to take them away, but they'd had other ideas.

'It was Dot's refusal to let us go and our promise to work really hard... Well, we were on our way,' she finished with a shrug.

'And now? Your goal of a consultancy is in sight, so what's next? Marriage and a family, like Cassie and Naomi?'

'Not for me,' she denied instantly, not even needing to think before she spoke. 'My independence is too important to me. If I only have myself to rely on, then I won't be let down.'

She'd been looking straight at Sam as she'd spoken or she'd never have seen the shadow that crossed his face. For just a second it looked like disappointment, but that could hardly be right. There was nothing personal between the two of them, in spite of the easy way they worked together. It must have been a memory of something in his past that she'd glimpsed.

'It would be a shame if you never married and had a family,' he said quietly as he straightened to his full height and slid a hand into his pocket to retrieve a set of keys. 'You would make a wonderful mother.'

His words seemed to taunt her, lingering in the room long after he'd gone. The expression in his eyes wouldn't go away either, so dark and so intent, although what had prompted him to say such a thing Kirstin couldn't imagine.

Out of necessity he'd had to develop an accurate knack for gauging the emotional suitability of their potential IVF mothers—it wasn't a road that all their childless couples were strong enough to travel. But his comment just now had sounded almost as if her own potential as a wife and mother was something to which he'd given equally careful consideration.

She shook her head at the ridiculous idea and quickly dismissed it, trying to force her mind back onto more rational things—such as checking the latest lab reports and entering the information on the relevant notes.

And if she still had some time free, there was always an enormous stack of books that she had to read, learn and inwardly digest in the next few months.

The trouble was, in spite of the fact that she had more than enough to occupy her mind, she still couldn't help thinking about the strange feeling that had been growing inside her all day. She didn't know what it was, only that it was making her feel... unsettled and edgy.

It was several hours later, when she was lying wide awake in her bed, wondering why sleep refused to come, that she realised what was causing it.

It wasn't that she was jealous of Naomi's happiness—she hoped that she wasn't that small-minded. To her dismay, she realised that she was jealous of the very fact that her friend was pregnant, that Naomi was going to have a child of her own.

CHAPTER TWO

KIRSTIN was still mulling over her startling discovery several days later. She'd lost hours of sleep over it and even found it dominating her thoughts at work.

That was the thing that worried her most. It had taken her years of single-minded dedication to get as far as she had in her chosen profession and she wasn't going to allow anything to jeopardise it at this stage.

This was the first time that anything had distracted her from her focus. Even the men she worked with were nothing more than colleagues, and the fact that she was surrounded all the time by women in all stages of their reproductive cycles didn't bother her— at least, it never had before Naomi had announced that she and Adam were expecting a baby.

Now all she could think about was how empty she felt, knowing she would probably never have a child of her own.

For the first time she could really empathise with the childless couples who attended the fertility clinic, knowing that it was probably their last hope for a family.

When the three of them had arrived at Dot's and Arthur's, they'd somehow managed to form their own special 'family'. Now that Cassie and Naomi were married, she was beginning to feel quite isolated. And for the first time there was no one she could talk to about the feelings welling up inside her. She could hardly talk to Dot about it, supportive and loyal though she was, because the last thing she wanted was to seem so mean and petty.

And that *wasn't* the issue.

It wasn't so much that she was jealous of what her two friends had so much as what she was missing out on. She had just discovered that there was an enormous gap in her life that she'd never even noticed before.

At least her job was fulfilling, she thought as she hurried to scrub up for Theatre to assist in a very unusual delivery. Thank goodness she was accustomed to working under supervision because today there were going to be a lot of eyes focused on the procedure. She was particularly thrilled that Sam had actually asked her to assist, even though it was in a minor capacity.

Her position as registrar in most hospital departments would have meant her being treated as a general dogsbody, spending horrendously long hours doing all the routine medical work associated with the patients on 'her' consultant's list.

She had been so lucky to secure a post under Sam Dysart, because he was as likely to visit each of his patients on a daily basis as she was. In fact, when she added up the number of hours he spent in Outpatients, following up on patients after operations, holding training sessions for the junior doctors and nurses *and* sitting on the various committees, she wondered how he ever found time to sleep.

'Good morning, everyone. This is Sarah Simmons,' Sam Dysart began in his deep, soothing voice as the anaesthetised woman's swollen abdomen was painted then draped in green cloths to leave only the operating field uncovered.

As usual, there was a completely separate team scrubbed and gowned for each of the patients in Theatre, with Adam Forrester leading the paediatrics team as Sam led his obs and gyn team.

This time, as Kirstin had expected, there were far more than the usual complement of staff in the theatre, and the exceptional operation was also being filmed for later teaching purposes. Thank goodness the mother-to-be wasn't carrying twins, she thought wryly. The theatre might have burst at the seams if they'd had to fit in a second paediatric team.

'She's twenty-seven years old and is thirty-five weeks pregnant with her first child,' Sam continued calmly. He was apparently completely oblivious of his unusually large audience as he watched a last ultrasound scan to check the relative positions of the baby's limbs.

'Everything all right at your end?' he asked 'Hal' Halawa, the anaesthetist, before holding his hand out for a scalpel to make his incision.

'On ultrasound, we picked up the fact several months ago that her child has a tumour growing in his throat. We have been monitoring the situation in the hope that it would grow slowly enough so that we could wait for him to be delivered normally.'

Kirstin listened to Sam's concise description of the situation while she buzzed the blood vessels to stop them bleeding then straightened up briefly while he made his initial tiny opening into the uterus.

The green drapes closest to Kirstin were instantly soaked in a gush of amniotic fluid in spite of the swabs positioned in readiness to absorb it.

'I don't want to lose any more of that than we need

to,' he murmured in an aside to Kirstin and the scrub nurse. 'It'll help to keep the little chap warm.'

He calmly slid two long fingers through the incision and positioned them between the stretched membrane and the enclosed child before he continued enlarging the incision, the precaution essential to make sure that the tender flesh of the baby wasn't cut at the same time.

'Unfortunately,' he continued aloud for the rest of his audience, 'the growth of the tumour has recently accelerated so that it is now completely crushing his windpipe. We have therefore opted to do an early Caesarean.'

Kirstin didn't need him to spell out the baby's chances without the innovative operation and neither did the rest of the observers.

Even if the baby had survived another five or so weeks in the womb with a rapidly enlarging tumour, delivery by natural childbirth wouldn't have been an option.

While his oxygen was being supplied by his mother, the fact that his windpipe was blocked didn't matter. Once he emerged from the womb at the end of labour, they would have been be left with less than a minute to clear his airway before the child started to suffer from lack of oxygen. That scenario would have meant certain brain damage, if not death itself.

This operation was a radical variation on a theme prompted by a desperate situation, and each person in the room knew it. If it hadn't been for the rhythmic bleeps and hisses of the support systems, you could have heard a pin drop while everyone waited for Sam to continue.

'To buy him, and us, some time,' he began again

when the bleeding from the second incision had been stemmed, 'we are going to deliver his head, neck and one arm through this incision, while leaving him still attached to the placenta to preserve the supply of oxygenated blood to his brain.'

Kirstin watched as his long fingers probed carefully through the gaping hole he had created and gently lifted the baby's head into view. One little arm followed as he positioned the child precisely for the next stage and attached the essential monitors.

It was so strange to see the little scrap lying there looking so pink and healthy but without his chest rising and falling with the regular evidence of life. He looked as if he were sleeping peacefully, the anaesthetic used to sedate his mother obviously having crossed the placenta to him.

'Now Adam will intubate him to make the airway useable,' Sam said, continuing his commentary as he stepped aside for the paediatric team. 'In this case, the rule of thumb is the rule of little finger as this is the most likely match for the right size of tube.'

Kirstin was smiling behind her mask as she watched Adam pretend to gauge the endotracheal tube against the tiny finger on the one visible little starfish hand.

She was surprised when she glanced up at Sam to find that his eyes were smiling, too, over the stark white of his mask. They gleamed dark brown at her under the bright lights as he shared the moment of humour with her.

She knew as well as he did that such an important item wouldn't have been left to last-minute guesswork, but would have been carefully measured from the pre-operation scan so that everything was readily to hand.

'How are they both doing?' Sam asked Hal over the soft murmur of laughter, and Kirstin was sorry that the brief moment of connection between the two of them had been broken.

'Both doing remarkably well,' the anaesthetist reported with a smile in his voice. 'His oxygen level hasn't fallen at all.'

'Excellent!' Sam exclaimed in satisfaction, and Kirstin knew he was commenting on those results and the way Adam had just slid the tube into position at the first attempt.

'Now fluid can be drained from the tumour to shrink it and buy the little chap some more time,' he continued in his clear soft rumble, having stepped aside until he was just behind Kirstin's shoulder to give the paediatric team some more room to manoeuvre.

Finally, half an hour after the whole procedure had begun, it was time to lift the tiny baby the whole way out of his warm nest and cut the umbilical cord.

The severing of the maternal link was the signal to his body to start the lifelong rhythm of breathing. As one, everyone stared intently, craning to look at the tiny child cradled safely in Sam's careful hands. When the little chest lifted with his first gasp of air a concerted sigh of relief and delight ran around the theatre. For Kirstin there was a special thrill at being even a minor part of the miracle and, as if he'd heard her thoughts, Sam's eyes met hers across the precious new life.

Sahru Ismail was waiting with the special crib, ready to whisk the baby down to the special care baby unit, and Kirstin couldn't help noticing the glances Hal was sending the stunningly beautiful nurse's way.

She vaguely remembered Naomi saying something about an attraction between their two colleagues. Was there another of those notorious doctor-nurse romances in the offing? she wondered, then shrugged off the sudden sweep of melancholy as she dragged her attention back to the work still going on.

'Do you feel up to doing a bit of embroidery?' Sam murmured as he took care of the afterbirth, his voice nearly inaudible under the buzz of excited conversation. 'Give the spectators a minute or two to disperse and you won't have to perform for a critical audience.'

A strange shiver worked its way up her spine, lifting all the tiny hairs under her theatre scrubs when she realised just how intently his dark gaze was focused on her.

Unwilling to speculate on the meaning of her reaction, Kirstin dismissed it as a result of the blast of cooler air let in by the departing bodies. The temperature in the theatre was usually fairly accurately controlled, but the press of extra bodies must have driven the heat up by several degrees. It couldn't possibly be anything to do with Sam's presence, or the strangely disembodied intensity of the expression in his eyes when half of the rest of his face was hidden behind a mask.

Pleased at the opportunity for extra practice, she smiled and nodded.

Not that she was short of practical work on his team. Sam was always very generous with his juniors, making sure they had plenty of chances to perfect their techniques while he was around to offer his skilled supervision and advice. He was definitely not a devotee of the 'see one, do one, teach one' school of medical education.

She was still glowing with his quiet word of praise for a job well done when she supervised Sarah Simmons's return to the department.

While Sarah had been in Theatre, her belongings had been transferred from one side of the unit to the other. This time, instead of being surrounded by other mums waiting for their babies to be born, she would be in the company of the other recently delivered mums and their new offspring.

'He *is* all right, isn't he?' the young woman demanded sleepily, still largely under the influence of the anaesthetic and completely oblivious of the fact that this had to be at least the tenth time she'd asked. 'He's alive?'

'He's very much alive,' Kirstin told her again, wondering if her words would finally register this time. 'He's small because he had to be born five weeks early, and he's in an incubator so we can give him extra oxygen if he needs it. But, other than that, he's perfect.'

Absolutely perfect, right down to his minute fingernails, she recalled with a sharp stab of remembered emotion.

She'd paid him a visit under the guise of checking up on him for his mother, glad that Sahru didn't know her well enough to question her motivation. If Cassie had been on duty she would have seen the turmoil going on inside her. She would have realised the truth—that for the first time her, oh, so pragmatic friend, Kirstin, hadn't been able to stay away.

She certainly wouldn't have been able to get away

with her nonchalant offer to hold the infant for a minute while the special sensor pad was placed under him in his cot without Cassie having passed some comment.

The little chap had still been dozy, too, and would be kept lightly sedated for a while for the sake of the unstable tissues in his throat. Even so, she'd caught a fleeting glimpse of dark navy eyes under tissue-thin lids while she'd marvelled anew at how fragile and bird-like his body felt.

'Each one of them is a tiny miracle,' Sahru had murmured as she'd settled her newest charge, and Kirstin had felt almost guilty as she'd avoided meeting her eyes, half-afraid that her thoughts would have been visible there.

How could she admit, even to herself, that after years of denying that she would ever want to marry, she was suddenly craving a family of her own?

'When can I see him?' Sarah asked, grabbing Kirstin's hand as though afraid she would leave without answering. At least it had the effect of attracting her wandering attention.

'You can go along to the special care baby unit as soon as you can stay awake long enough not to fall out of a wheelchair,' Kirstin teased. 'I realise you're not going to believe anything but your own eyes, but here's something to be going on with.'

She produced the instant photograph which was becoming a regular feature of the liaison between the SCBU and Obs and Gyn.

It was several moments before her patient could control the weak tears that slid down her cheeks, the precious photo cradled gingerly between trembling hands.

'He's so little,' she whispered brokenly as she used one hand to brush away the tears then sank back, exhausted, against the pillows. 'And he nearly didn't get this far…'

'Shall I just prop the picture up on top of your locker where you can see it without it getting crushed?' Kirstin suggested when she realised the young woman would be asleep again at any moment. She paused briefly to have a last look at the photo herself, marvelling at the complexity of the little boy's birth and the outstanding success of it.

Now it was just a case of waiting for the full lab report on the fluid removed from the tumour and formulating a treatment protocol. The only thing she could be certain of was that the majority of laryngeal tumours were benign. That being so, having survived such an unusual delivery, the little chap should soon have every chance of a long and healthy life.

Unlike her, if she didn't catch up on some of the mountain of paperwork waiting for completion. There were several of Sam's patients due to be released today and it was her job to make certain that their records were up to date. Then there were reports to be written for their GPs' records and others for the health visitors who would be checking up on them and their babies at intervals once they returned home.

Kirstin grabbed a cup of coffee before she set off towards the office with an armful of files, pulling a face when she estimated just how long the mountain was going to take to scale. Much of the repetitious paperwork could now be computer-generated, with extra copies of a report available at the press of a button. But with each pregnancy and delivery so different, it was vital to get the little details correct, and that meant concentration.

'How's she doing?' prompted a familiar voice, jerking her out of her thoughts and back to the present, narrowly escaping a slop of hot coffee over her wrist. It was more by luck than judgement that she hung onto the stack of files clutched against her white coat.

'Sam! You made me jump,' she complained, suddenly breathless when she realised that she'd nearly cannoned into him, then embarrassed that she'd used his first name. It was something she'd consciously avoided, particularly with male colleagues, when she'd first started her medical training. It had started as a deliberate attempt to keep her distance, and it had quickly become a habit.

At least it had been until the last few days...ever since Naomi had announced her pregnancy.

For some unaccountable reason, the barrier of distance between herself and the rest of the world seemed to have developed a crack. Since then, she'd found herself thinking of the man as Sam, rather than Mr Dysart, and now she'd even used his name aloud.

And he'd noticed, she realised with a renewed sweep of heat across her cheeks. She could see it in the quizzical lift of one dark eyebrow, a trademark of his, and the intent expression in his eyes.

Belatedly, she scrambled to recall his question.

'Mrs Simmons is doing well,' she reported formally, and noted the fugitive gleam of amusement with chagrin. She wasn't fooling him. He was far too bright not to have noticed her slip, or realised that she was trying to duck back behind the safety of that protective wall.

That didn't stop her trying to re-establish the distance between them. 'She initially came out of the anaesthetic quite quickly and her vital signs were good so she didn't stay in Post-Op very long. We've now got her settled on the ward but between dozes she's asking how soon she can go down and see her baby.'

'As soon as you're happy she's ready for it,' Sam confirmed in a gratifying show of confidence in her judgement. She was grateful, too, that he seemed willing to go along with her pretence that nothing had changed. 'And next time she surfaces, you can give her the good news. The lab confirmed that her baby's tumour is benign.'

'Thank goodness,' Kirstin breathed in relief. It would have been a tragedy if, after such a fraught arrival into the world, the tiny child had had to embark on a desperate fight to stay here. 'So it'll just mean waiting until he's recovered enough from the birth before he has surgery to remove the rest of it properly?'

'Basically, yes. From the position of it, it should even be possible to do it endoscopically,' he agreed. 'Mind you, I don't envy whoever gets the job of operating inside a throat that small.'

'But at least that way he'll end up without a visible scar,' she pointed out. 'No one need ever know how close he came to missing out on life, unless he tells them.'

'Any problems for me?' He smiled, his expression even more potent without the mask though she silently castigated herself for even thinking it.

What on earth was wrong with her these days that she was so aware of the man? She should be concentrating on what he was saying rather than the expression in his eyes as he said it.

'None for you, but a mountain of paperwork for me to do,' Kirstin replied, glancing pointedly at her armful of files as she voiced her perennial complaint. 'Sometimes it feels as if I spend more time writing about medicine than practising it.'

'You think *you've* got the rough end of the stick?' he challenged. 'Wait till you get your consultancy. They start shovelling it even higher then. Apart from the basic paperwork relating to patients, there are department policy meetings, hospital policy meetings, department finance meetings, planning and implementation meetings, etc., etc. Then a great pile of bumph will arrive on your desk a couple of days later to remind you of every word everyone said at each meeting.'

'So you're saying it wasn't worth working so hard to become a consultant?' she retorted, throwing his challenge right back at him. Suddenly she felt almost electrically alive to be crossing verbal swords with him like this. It was a revelation, something she'd never felt before.

'Oh, I didn't say that,' he said softly, the gleam in his eyes different now. 'It was worth every minute of it to be able to do that operation today, to know that I was capable of doing it and saving both of them.'

Kirstin was so struck by the amount of emotion in his voice that she was seized with the mad longing to throw her arms around him and give him a hug.

That would certainly be going a step too far, she thought as she took half a step backwards to remove herself from temptation. This was unknown territory. She'd never felt such a strong desire for physical contact before and wasn't certain that she liked it. Safer by far to concentrate on the goals that had dominated the last nine years of her life.

'That's what I thought,' she said quietly, relieved when she found she could still mentally slot him into his 'senior colleague' niche. 'And that means I must get on with this heap, or I'll never make it.'

They went their separate ways and she settled down to the dreaded task, but just because Sam Dysart was out of sight it didn't mean that he was out of mind. How could he be when each file had a regular parade of his familiar signature punctuating changes in treatment or dosages of drugs?

She looked at the strong black swirls of his intertwined initials and realised that she'd never really seen what his writing looked like. Every entry on the chart was carefully added, usually in a different hand each time, witness to the way he always dictated the changes he wanted to whichever member of staff accompanied him, then read them over and initialled them.

'No point sitting here admiring the wretched things,' she muttered as she reined in her wandering thoughts. 'Get on with it while you've got the time free, or you'll still be doing it at midnight.'

She took a fortifying mouthful of coffee and made a start.

Sam was a nice man, a kind man, and so very good at his job, Kirstin thought as she watched him show a couple out of his consulting room a couple of days later.

Today had been set aside for the next round of interviews and tests with the latest prospective candidates for assisted pregnancies. Each patient would initially have been referred to the special clinic by their general practitioner or their gynaecologist if they attended a hospital without such a specialist unit.

In a minute the rest of the team would convene for their fortnightly meeting to compare notes on their findings and recommendations.

She didn't know whether this was the way similar departments in other hospitals worked, but the more she learned about Sam Dysart's methods, the more she liked them. The only trouble was, in spite of the fact that all their potential candidates shared a problem with having children, not all of them were suitable for inclusion in the programme.

Initially, she'd easily accepted the fact that some couples were never going to be able achieve their goal, but that was changing and today was the first time she'd found herself dreading the meeting.

Ever since she'd had to admit to herself that she wanted a child of her own, she seemed to have developed a greater empathy with the patients who were left without hope.

She'd found herself drawing parallels with her own situation. If she continued concentrating on her career, how would she react if one day she found she'd left it too late?

What would it be like to know that she was never going to be able to experience the mixture of joy and discomfort as her body nurtured a growing foetus? How would she cope with the fact that there would never be a child to call her 'Mummy' and depend on her for protection and guidance? How difficult would it be to accept that when she died there would be nothing left of her to mark her presence in the world?

Until recently, she'd never even contemplated the possibility that she might want to have a baby. Her decision not to marry had been made so long ago that it was a part of the very fabric of her life, and the consequences had seemed irrelevant.

Then Naomi had announced her pregnancy and the world had somehow turned topsy-turvy.

'Right, if everyone's ready, let's start with John and Dianne,' Sam said to the room at large, and Kirstin hoped that the feelings she hastily pushed into a back corner of her mind would stay there. Her own emotions had no place in this meeting.

'This couple has been married for seven years,' Sam continued, giving his usual very brief case history as he sat at the head of the table. 'In that time they've never used any form of contraception but Dianne's never become pregnant in spite of the fact that her periods are regular.

'After an examination and the usual advice about thermometers, and so on, her GP did a series of blood tests to check her hormone levels, establishing that she appears to be ovulating normally. Obviously, that doesn't guarantee that the eggs she's producing are viable. There's no evidence of endocrine disorder, or any disease of heart or lungs. Although she had some infections in her late teens and early twenties, she hasn't had any abdominal operations.

'John was checked and was found to be producing sperm of sufficient quantity and quality to effect fertilisation.'

He gestured towards his neighbour in a time-honoured ritual, almost like passing the baton in a relay race.

'The laparoscopy showed a normal healthy uterus

and two normal healthy ovaries, but both Fallopian tubes are badly scarred, possibly as the result of infections following some amateur waterskiing in her late teens and early twenties.'

The baton passed on.

'Her other blood work showed no problems with anaemia or infections and she appears to be a good candidate—relatively young, fit and active.'

'But most of all, determined,' Sam interposed, then turned towards the psychologist on the team. 'Do you agree?'

'Definitely,' Leslie Finch said with a smile. 'Obviously, we're limited in the amount of time we can spend getting to know them, but there were no over-the-top histrionics about their lives being ruined for want of their own genetic offspring. Just a bone-deep certainty that they would go through hell and high water if it would help Dianne to get pregnant. I was really impressed with them, both individually and as a couple. I wish more people were as supportive of each other as they are.'

'Any one else with any comments or questions?' Sam threw the discussion open and Kirstin raised a hand.

'Determination is essential, but what about their attitude to the possibility of failure?'

'Good point,' Leslie conceded. 'Far too many people still go into IVF thinking it's going to solve all their problems. Even when we try to tell them that the success rate can be as low as fourteen per cent on a first attempt, they still automatically believe that they'll be one of the lucky ones.'

'And John and Dianne?' Kirstin prompted.

'As Sam said, they're determined to give it a really

good go, but not to the point where Dianne's health would be put at risk. I will, of course, be meeting with them at intervals during the treatment to reassess the situation.'

Kirstin could well understand how the stresses of such a procedure could induce a whole new level of marital strife. She'd already seen instances of it since she started work in the unit and had also seen the benefit of the local branch of the support group for infertile couples. Sometimes all it seemed to take was the knowledge that others were going through exactly the same traumas to take the pressure off.

'Well, if there are no other questions, I'd like to put them on the list,' Sam said with his trademark raised eyebrow. 'We can send them confirmation and get them to phone in to sort out the first available date to start the hormone injections.'

Depending on Dianne's response to the mixture of hormones in each daily injection, they could go on for anything from seven to twelve days before the ovaries had been sufficiently stimulated to produce a crop of ripe eggs. Kirstin wouldn't be involved in giving the injections, but she would be checking the results of the daily blood tests and ultrasound scans to make absolutely certain that Dianne didn't start to become dangerously over-stimulated.

Her next direct contact with Dianne would be when she came in for the ripe eggs to be harvested, but that could be weeks or even months down the road.

'Next. Anna and Tom,' Sam announced, and Kirstin's quiet pleasure at the thought of John's and Dianne's acceptance on the programme swiftly faded. She had some worrying doubts about this next couple, but no concrete proof of her concerns.

She watched Sam carefully as he did his usual run-through and was relieved to note the tell-tale signs that he wasn't completely happy either.

Her insight was rewarded when, instead of handing the baton on around the table in his usual way, he glanced around the group first with a frown pleating his forehead.

'I know this couple is close to the upper limit that the local health authority will agree to fund, but there's something…not quite right,' he said in the end. 'Did any of you pick up on it?'

'I think…well, I'm almost certain,' Kirstin began hesitantly, then took the bull by the horns. 'Earlier on, while they were waiting to be called in for their interview with you, they were sitting together talking in the waiting room. I'd just had to take a phone call in the office and I don't think they realised I'd come into the room.'

It wasn't as if she'd deliberately been creeping around to catch people out. Her soft-soled shoes would have made virtually no noise on the hard-wearing carpet used to soften the sounds surrounding the waiting room.

'She was getting quite agitated about something and he was trying to calm her down, but, instead of saying Anna, he was calling her Marion. It could have been a family nickname but for some reason it rang a bell so I went and checked up on the long case history form—the one where we ask about family members and familial illnesses.'

Sam nodded. It was necessarily a very comprehensive list of questions, an attempt to rule out pitfalls due to genetically linked fertility problems.

'Go on,' he invited.

'On the original form, Anna gave her own age as thirty-eight and her older sister's name as Marion and her age as forty-five. I've got a feeling that the person we know as Anna is really Marion, and that she's pretending to be her younger sister to trick her way onto the programme.'

Apart from the fact that the younger sister would have an eleven per cent chance of success and the older one little more than four per cent, there was also the worrying increased risk of problems such as Down's syndrome to consider. That was apart from the dangers of basing treatment for one sister on the medical records of the other.

There was a surprised silence for a moment, then everyone started talking at once.

'Are you certain, Kirstin?' Sam's voice cut through the hubbub.

'Pretty much,' she confirmed. 'But is there some way you can check up with her GP before you say anything? Perhaps the two sisters have a different blood group or something? A scar from an operation?'

'We'll shelve the rest of the discussion on that case until we've clarified the situation,' he said decisively.

'That would certainly go a long way to explaining why I felt they were holding back all the time,' the psychologist said with a wry smile. 'Well spotted.'

The meeting continued but if she was honest, Kirstin had to admit that she was distracted by her own thoughts.

It must be dreadful to be so desperate to have a child that you would lie to be accepted as a patient, even risking your own health by pretending to be your younger sister. The fact that the local health authority could end up wasting a great deal of money when attempt after attempt failed when those funds could have been successfully used on several younger women was only one of the factors they had obviously rejected.

While she knew that such a deception was wrong, she still couldn't help feeling a little sorry for the couple.

That in turn made her wonder if she was the sort of person who could be driven to those sorts of extremes. If she reached her mid-forties still childless, would she be tempted to twist the system for her own ends, regardless of the dangers to her own health?

CHAPTER THREE

'NAOMI FORRESTER,' Kirstin called with a broad grin on her face. 'Would you like to come straight in?'

It was the first antenatal appointment for her friend and she was taking great delight in teasing her, pretending that she was just another patient.

'Is it my turn, now, Doctor?' Naomi asked with an innocent expression as she followed her through to the examination room. It was a good job the midwife knew that the two of them had been friends for years or she would have wondered what they were playing at.

'How are you feeling?' Kirstin asked, dropping the joke as she closed the door. 'Are you being very sick?'

'How can you tell?' Naomi said with a groan as she deposited her belongings and slipped her shoes off, before climbing on the scales. 'Was it the permanent green tint to my face that gave it away?'

'How bad is it, honestly?' Kirstin prompted, concerned for her friend. 'How much are you managing to keep down? Are you in danger of dehydration? I could give you something to help.'

Kirstin knew that she could trust Naomi to be sensible. There was no way that she would do anything to risk her own health, let alone that of her child.

'Honestly? So far, I'm coping,' she admitted with a grimace. 'I don't want to take anything unnecessarily, but if it gets any worse, I might take you up on the offer—at least to take something to stop the vomiting.'

Kirstin entered Naomi's weight into the appropriate column in the computer file then turned back to check her blood pressure.

It was all routine stuff, generally completed before patients with a problem were shown through to her. But this was Naomi and she felt almost compelled to perform the checks herself.

'Everything seems completely normal so far, unless there's anything you're worried about?'

'Only about getting disgustingly fat.'

'Well, you don't need to worry about that at the moment. If your pre-pregnancy weight is accurate, you haven't put on more than a couple of ounces yet, and you've nearly completed your first trimester.'

'You wait!' Naomi predicted dolefully. 'Once I stop feeling so rotten, my appetite will come back with a vengeance and I'll raise eating for two to the level of an Olympic sport!'

'Chance would be a fine thing!' Kirstin grumbled. 'You and Cassie have always been able to eat whatever you wanted without worrying about putting on weight. *I'm* the one with the sweet tooth who has to watch every mouthful.'

'Who are you trying to kid?' Naomi countered heatedly. 'You lost all that extra weight years ago, round about the same time you put on that growth spurt and left the two of us behind. You've got legs up to your armpits now, and not a spare ounce anywhere. You never sit down long enough to put on weight.'

Kirstin snorted her disbelief but loved Naomi for her loyalty, biased though it was. She'd always known the truth—that she was nothing special. Why else had people found it so easy to pass her on without a second thought?

'Anyway,' Naomi added briskly as she retrieved her shoes, 'I can't take up all your time when you've got another patient waiting.'

'Another patient?' Kirstin tapped a key to bring the list up on the computer. 'There's nothing here. You were my last one this time.'

'No. I'm certain I saw someone else waiting to see you. Shall I send them in?'

Kirstin was frowning, wondering what had gone wrong with the state-of-the-art system that it could swallow up patients without a trace, when she heard the familiar sound of her two friends' conspiratorial chuckles.

'Cassie! Come in!' she invited as she gave a silent sigh of relief. Thank goodness there wasn't anything wrong with the computer after all. Practical jokes she could cope with, especially after the years of practice with these two. 'Have you come to grill Naomi to find out how she's doing?'

'Partly,' Cassie admitted with a mysterious smile. 'But I'd also like you to do a test for me.'

'Test?' Kirstin echoed weakly, suddenly filled with a strange feeling as though she were viewing the scene through a room filled with crazy mirrors. Everything seemed to be peculiarly distorted as if it were being repeated over and over again.

'Well, I did one of the home tests this morning, but I just want to be certain that it wasn't a false positive.' Her smile was almost blinding in its excitement and happiness.

'*You're* pregnant as well!'

Thank goodness she was too stunned to say more. It would have been unforgivable if her words had matched the yawning void that had opened up inside her.

'Isn't it fantastic?' Naomi exclaimed, looking as pleased as though she were a conjurer pulling rabbits out of a hat. 'Both of us pregnant at once, and the babies due within a month of each other. Dot is going to be over the moon.'

Kirstin smiled but it was difficult when breathing was an effort.

She was pleased for her two friends, she really was. They were getting everything they'd always wanted, and all in such a very short time.

So why did she feel as if something were slowly dying inside her? She was equally as lucky as they were. Her dreams were all coming true, too, so what was the matter with her? Why wasn't she as excited as Cassie and Naomi were?

Suddenly she realised that it had been an awfully long time since Naomi's question. Thank goodness she and Cassie were so busy bubbling over with excited plans that they hadn't noticed. The last thing she wanted was to have to go into any explanations about her distraction, and this certainly wasn't the time or the place to sort through her chaotic emotions.

She pasted a brighter smile on her face but before she could find any suitable words there was a brief knock at the door.

'Come in,' she called, ashamed to feel grateful for the reprieve. Perhaps by the time she'd dealt with whoever it was she'd have her head back together.

'Oh, I'm sorry, Kirstin, I thought you'd finished,' Sam said in quick apology and made to withdraw.

'Don't go,' Naomi called. 'She has finished, really. Cassie and I were ganging up on her to break some news.'

'Good news, I presume, if your expressions are anything to go by.'

'The best,' Naomi agreed. 'Cassie and I are both pregnant.'

'That's what I like to hear—members of staff doing their best to keep my department busy,' he teased. 'When are you due?'

'*She* got pregnant on her honeymoon,' taunted Cassie, clearly delighted to be able to make Naomi blush.

'You weren't slow off the mark either,' Naomi retorted swiftly. 'We're due within a couple of weeks of each other and you weren't married that long ago.'

Kirstin felt as if her face were going to crack if she had to keep smiling much longer. It would have been all right if Naomi and Cassie had continued their conversation with Sam, but he seemed intent on bringing her into the discussion.

'I see what you meant about the three of you being closer than most sisters,' he commented. One dark brown eyebrow curved upwards as he looked from the animated pair to Kirstin sitting with one hip hitched on the corner of the examination table.

'Well, we have known each other since we were fifteen,' Cassie pointed out.

'You're certainly keeping up the togetherness. Two of you married within a few months of each other and then expecting your babies just a few weeks apart.' He turned to Kirstin. 'It must be your turn any minute.'

'Not me,' Kirstin denied swiftly, the way she always did. Except this time she was unsettled to feel a pang of sadness as she heard herself say it.

'She's the confirmed career-woman,' Cassie offered with a smile. 'She's always said she'd rather concentrate on getting her consultancy.'

Sam was silent for a moment and when Kirstin saw the thoughtful frown drawing those dark brows together she wished Cassie hadn't said anything. Sam was the sort of person who saw more deeply than most, and after the confidences she'd spilled the other day she was afraid he might to be able to tell how confused she was.

'I hope you've thought carefully about the consequences of that decision,' Sam said quietly, his dark eyes strangely intent on hers for several seconds.

Kirstin's heart stumbled for a single beat before it suddenly began to race, almost as if it was reacting to danger.

What was going on behind those thoughtful eyes? It was as if he were really seeing her for the first time, as if he were trying to get inside her mind, the way he did so successfully with their patients.

'What time are you off duty today?' Naomi asked, and Kirstin suddenly realised that she'd been holding her breath while Sam had been gazing at her. She drew in a quivering lungful of air as she turned to face her friend, frantically cudgelling her brain to remember what time her shift had started.

'I won't finish until nine tonight,' she finally replied. 'Why?'

'We're driving down together to visit Dot to give her the news,' Naomi said.

'Luke and Adam are going with us,' Cassie added. 'Are you sure you won't be able to come?'

Out of the corner of her eye Kirstin caught a move-ment and realised that Sam was still following the conversation. Their eyes met and the quizzical ex-pression on his face told her that he was considering offering to cover the last part of her shift.

She stared fiercely at him and when she gave a tiny shake of her head he subsided to lean back against the edge of the desk. It would have been a thoughtful gesture on his part, but she was actually quite relieved not to be part of the evening's celebrations.

She'd been feeling more and more like an outsider ever since Cassie had got married, and after today's information she was feeling almost totally isolated.

Anyway, Sam had probably been working longer than she had, and taking on part of a junior's shift on top of that wasn't a good idea.

'Make sure you give Dot my love,' she instructed as she got to her feet and straightened her white coat. 'Tell her I'll be down to see her as soon as I get a couple of days off together. Then I'll be able to spend the night and we can really have time to talk.'

Perhaps by then she'd have been able to get her head straight. If she hadn't, Dot would probably be the only one who could untangle her thoughts—if she dared to tell them.

'Hey, are you shoving us out without doing that test for me?' Cassie demanded. 'I can hardly an-nounce it to Dot if I haven't actually had the preg-nancy officially confirmed.'

Sam chuckled, too, his deep masculine tone a har-monious counterpoint.

To Kirstin's surprise, he stayed chatting to Naomi about her work on the paediatric ward while she buzzed in and out dealing with Cassie. He was still there, apparently quite happy to while away a few minutes in the middle of a busy shift, when her two friends set off along the corridor arm in arm, their feet obviously still hardly touching the floor.

'I'm so sorry you were kept waiting like that,' she apologised hurriedly, suddenly remembering that he hadn't come there to socialise. 'I hope it wasn't something urgent?'

'No. Nothing urgent,' he said dismissively as he settled his hips on the edge of the desk again and folded his arms comfortably across his enviably flat belly. 'Just to tell you that your suspicions were right about Marion pretending to be her sister Anna to get on the IVF programme. She also lied about her age because she'll be fifty in just a few weeks.'

'I hope I look that good at fifty,' Kirstin exclaimed in surprise. 'She really does look as if she could pass for someone a dozen years younger. If I hadn't overheard them talking…'

'Unfortunately, we can't take her young-looking exterior as a sign that her reproductive system is similarly youthful.' Sam sighed.

'So what will happen to them now? She was trying to obtain expensive treatment by deception. Will they be in trouble with the law?'

'Not on my account,' he said firmly. 'It will be bad enough for them when they're told they aren't being accepted on the IVF programme. I don't intend bringing heavy-handed bureaucracy down on them as well.'

'Were you their last hope?' She could see from the compassion in his eyes that he hated disappointing desperate people, too. She was feeling almost guilty for having uncovered the deception.

'Probably, unless they've got the money to go abroad for treatment. There are some centres elsewhere in the world where they'll accept women right into their mid-fifties and even beyond.'

Kirstin remembered something Dot had said once and chuckled. 'I was told that the reason God didn't let women over fifty have babies was because they'd put them down somewhere and forget where they'd left them.'

Sam chuckled, too, the husky sound rich in the quiet oasis of the consulting room, then his expression grew serious again.

'Kirstin, that's partly why I was concerned when your friend said you'd decided not to marry and have children,' he said quietly. 'You've probably noticed that quite a number of our IVF patients trying for a first baby are former career-women.'

'Not that many,' Kirstin countered defensively. 'You've got a complete cross-section of all types of women coming to the unit.'

'Most of whom have been trying to start a family almost from the beginning of their marriages,' he pointed out logically. 'This means that by the time they realise they've got a problem, they're still young enough for us to have a good chance of helping them. The career-women, on the other hand, are getting to their mid-thirties and suddenly changing their minds about their decision to forgo a family. By the time *they* realise there's a problem, their fertility level is starting to drop off fast and we're into a race against time.'

Kirstin pulled a face as she nodded. She knew he was right.

'That's why I said I hoped you had thought about

your decision carefully,' he continued. 'The cut-off date can arrive very quickly for a woman who puts things off too long. A man who makes such a decision still has a lot of years in which to change his mind.'

Kirstin knew that what he was saying was no more than the truth. She wondered what he would say if he knew how many doubts she'd been having ever since Naomi had announced her pregnancy. No doubt her middle-of-the-night soul-searching would go even deeper with the extra incentive of Cassie's news.

He was watching her while the thoughts ran around inside her head, apparently unworried by her long silence, and she recognised it as a trait she'd seen often when he'd faced patients with difficult decisions. She'd been working with him for several months now, and never once had he given the impression that he was in a hurry.

Suddenly she found herself looking at him in the light of his own words. With his seniority, he must be about thirty-five by now and, if the hospital grapevine was to be believed, had never been married.

Had the conviction she'd heard in his tone been evidence that *he* had reached the stage of reconsidering an earlier decision of his own?

He was obviously highly intelligent and completely dedicated and probably already had more degrees than a thermometer. Someone in his financial position with no dependent ex-wife and children would be considered quite a catch, especially one who had already risen to such dizzy heights that he was in charge of such a specialised unit.

But perhaps she was leaping to conclusions. The hospital grapevine wasn't infallible and suddenly she had an unexpectedly urgent need to know more about him.

'What about you?' she heard herself saying, her voice taking on an almost challenging tone in the quiet room. 'Did you decide not to have children, or is there someone…?'

Her voice tailed off into horrified silence when she realised just what she'd done. It was one thing to quiz her colleagues during a chat over a cup of coffee, but to speak like that to *him*…

She could have bitten her tongue out—*should* have bitten it out rather than open her mouth when her thoughts were so muddled. This was the man who would soon be deciding whether to accept her application for a permanent position on the staff in his department.

Her cheeks were burning and she didn't dare look at him. If he took offence…

'There was someone, once,' he said quietly, and the resignation in his voice drew her eyes up to meet his.

There was such sadness in their dark depths that her unruly tongue took over again.

'You wanted to marry her?' she asked, wondering why the thought of Sam Dysart in love with that unknown woman tied something inside her in knots.

He shrugged, his broad shoulders lifting the fine cloth of his suit jacket just once. 'She didn't want… It didn't work out,' he finished simply. 'And then I became involved with work in the IVF field. It doesn't leave much time free for relationships and commitment.'

Kirstin hadn't been able to help noticing how often the man was still in the department long after he should have gone off duty. For the first time she found herself wondering if he stayed because there was nothing important to go home to.

'But what about a family?' she asked. 'You spend all your time helping other people to have children. Don't you ever think about having some of your own?'

'I did, once, but...not any more.'

There was an audible catch in his voice and she could have wept when she saw the desolation he tried to hide.

He might have been saying that he'd decided against having children, but she was almost certain that wasn't how he felt. She only had to see the gentle, caring way he handled their tiny charges to know that he would be a wonderful father. What on earth had happened to make him give up on the idea, especially when he was so determined to get her to reconsider her own decision?

She never knew whether she'd have found out if she'd have blurted out yet another intrusive question because the comparative peace of the room was broken by the all-too-familiar sound of a pager.

'Yours or mine?' Sam quipped as they both reached for their gadgets. Hers was clipped to the pocket of her white coat and was mercifully blank.

His was attached to the dark leather belt circling his lean waist, and he groaned when he tilted it up and read the contact number.

'It's Marion, alias Anna, again,' he said with a grimace. 'She was notified this morning that we couldn't accept her on the programme and that must be the fifth call today already. She seems to think that badgering me is going to get her what she wants.'

'She probably guessed that there's a soft centre underneath that professional shell,' Kirstin dared to tease, and saw him blink.

'Whether or not I've got a soft centre doesn't come into it,' he said with a trace of colour spreading over the lean planes of his cheeks. 'The plain facts of the case are that she's too old for IVF to be able to promise her any sort of odds on success, so I'm not permitted to offer it to her.'

'And on top of that, there are all the increased risks to the health of the older mother,' Kirstin added, feeling that he needed to know that she was in agreement with him. 'Very few women appreciate how risky pregnancy is even for the young fit and healthy—one of the most dangerous things they'll ever do, unless they're into bungee jumping or rodeo riding.'

'Is that one of the reasons you've crossed it off your list?' he asked offhandedly, as if her answer didn't really matter at all.

Either he wasn't hiding his thoughts as well as usual or she was getting better at reading him, and it was the intensity in his eyes that prompted her into an unaccustomed burst of simple honesty.

'Actually, it's not so much having children that I've ruled out as marriage,' she announced quietly, then stopped short. Any minute now she was going to be telling him about all her late-night deliberations and her unexpected longing for a child of her own.

That would never do, especially when he would be the one ultimately in control of her continued employment in the obs and gyn unit. How much good would it do her chances of landing a permanent post if she told him that she was thinking of embarking on the route to single parenthood?

She made her escape on the pretext that he would want her to go while he spoke yet again to Marion, but it was more to escape his clear, analytical gaze. It was almost as if she were expecting him to be able to read her guilty conscience.

Because that *was* what she was thinking of doing, she admitted silently as she made her way back towards the ward.

Her determination not to embark on marriage was unchanged, but the more she thought about having a child, the more she was realising that it was a real possibility. In fact, so much of her present situation was in favour of it that she might almost have been subconsciously preparing for it.

Take her new flat, for instance. There had been two available in the same converted Victorian house, and for some unaccountable reason she'd chosen the one on the ground floor with easy access to a secluded walled garden. It would be a perfect home in which to bring up a child.

Her financial situation was good, too. Even if she hadn't been within months of her next increase in salary, she was already paid as much as many male colleagues who had wives and families to support.

Then there was the wonderful crèche facility that St Augustine's had set up for staff, so she wouldn't be stuck looking for suitable care for a child when she returned to work.

And her child certainly wouldn't lack for company, with Naomi's and Cassie's babies on their way and little Jenny, already on her feet, on hand to play big sister…

Her rosy deliberations were interrupted by a voice

calling her name somewhere behind her. She turned to find Hal hurrying after her.

'Hello, Hal.' She perched on the window-sill overlooking a view of damp, muddy lawns and winter-bare trees with only the hint of spring-flowering crocuses around their feet. 'What are you doing here? It's a bit early for you to be doing your rounds of the pre-operative patients, isn't it?'

The young Egyptian anaesthetist gave her one of his sweet smiles, the dark colour of his skin showing his white teeth to perfection.

'I was hoping to have a quick word with you about Sahru,' he said after a glance in either direction to make certain they couldn't be overheard. 'Have you got a minute to spare?'

'Of course I have. Do you want to find an empty room somewhere?' she offered.

'That won't be necessary,' he said quickly. 'I just wanted to know if you would be willing to have a word with her about the possibilities of having an operation.'

'An operation? But surely she needs to see Sam for that. I'm only his registrar,' she reminded him.

'I know this. Sahru did agree to see Sam several months ago, but she still hasn't made an appointment. It's difficult for her. But you are a woman, and this will make it easier for Sahru to tell you about her problem. Then, if you agree that she should see Sam, she will want you to be with her for the appointment.'

Kirstin was intrigued but, knowing of Sahru Ismail's Sudanese origins, she had a fair idea what was going to be involved.

'Is there anything you think I ought to know before I see her?' she asked warily. 'If she wants to keep everything fairly quiet, I could find a way to keep her name out of my diary until we know where things are going.'

'If you can, that would be good. But I think the only thing that is really important is that she knows that I love her and want to marry her,' he said firmly. 'She is so concerned about the severity of her problem that she will not agree that we have a future. So she is expecting that when you see her you will agree with her, while I am hoping that you will be able to find some way to help her.'

Kirstin noted how careful Hal was being not to mention exactly what Sahru's problem was, but she was in no doubt. The only thing she was worried about was the severity of the problem, and if Sahru was this adamant it must be bad.

'For both your sakes, it would probably be a good idea if I see her as soon as possible,' she advised. 'When is she next off duty?'

Hal consulted the piece of paper with a list of Sahru's shifts and Kirstin quickly suggested a suitable time. It would mean coming in early the next day to see her before her own duty started, but that was better than chancing the young woman's nerves getting the better of her and frightening her off.

'Kirstin, I am very grateful that you will do this,' Hal said quietly as he shook her hand in an oddly formal gesture of farewell. 'I have promised to give her the time of the appointment and have told her that I have confidence in both your word and your skill in diagnosis.'

Kirstin was deeply touched by his compliments, knowing they weren't something he gave lightly, and hoped she would be able to live up to them. In the meantime, she would have to have a quick word with Sam to let him know what she had agreed to.

She tried to tell herself that the only reason she wanted to speak to the man was because she didn't want to find herself on the wrong side of departmental policy. There was no way she was going to admit, even to herself, that she was beginning to look for excuses to spend time with him.

It was several extremely busy hours before she saw Sam again: hours in which she'd seen two mothers delivered of beautiful babies; hours in which her desire for a child of her own had grown beyond mere longing.

Unfortunately, the fact that her woman's brain was capable of working on several problems simultaneously was a disadvantage at times like these.

She'd been busy dealing with a malpresentation of a twin. At the same time a woman who'd waited until she'd already entered the second stage of labour opted at full volume for an epidural delivery. That still didn't stop her brain from gnawing away at her own dilemma.

There was a newly qualified midwife on duty who was honest enough to admit that she would welcome some assistance.

'I've read about these presentations, but I've never had to deal with one before,' she confessed out of earshot of the mother.

'I had one similar to this shortly after I started my residency,' Kirstin consoled her. 'I was lucky to have Sam Dysart on hand to bring the book-learning to life, so I'll try to do the same for you.

'In the meantime,' she muttered through clenched

teeth as a blood-curdling stream of profanity emanated from the other delivery suite, 'I'm going to do
a quick check on our vocal mum to find out how far
she's progressed. I don't know if there'll be enough
time for a shot of pethidine to help her. If not,' she
added wickedly, 'I'll suggest your colleague encour-
ages her to keep the Entonox mask on to see if that'll
cut down on the volume a bit.'

Kirstin returned just as the young midwife was
checking on the second baby's progress. They'd
hoped that it would turn before delivery, but it obviously wasn't going to happen now. The first child, a
perfect little boy weighing nearly as much as most
single births, was already wrapped up warmly and
waiting for his sibling to join him. Now she could see
a pair of tiny feet and knew that it was just a matter
of waiting patiently for enough of the baby to pro-
trude so that she could assist the delivery of the head.

'Perfect timing,' the young midwife murmured
when she returned, glancing up to check that Kirstin
was drawing on a fresh pair of gloves before she
stepped aside.

As Kirstin had expected, the little girl emerging
inch by inch had both arms upraised, still firmly inside the mother. As soon as the lower edge of the
anterior shoulder was showing, it was time to move
as quickly as possible. The head was now in the
mother's pelvis and would be pressing on the umbilical cord. Any delay could starve the infant of essential blood.

'Baby is too large for Bracht's method, so we'll try
Muller's,' she said softly as she supported the slippery
body with both hands and pulled it steeply down towards the bed. She heard her young colleague give a

sigh of relief when the anterior arm and shoulder appeared, then she reversed the procedure, lifting the infant up to free the other arm and shoulder.

Kirstin gently rotated the baby so that she was 'facing' the bed while the midwife positioned herself to apply downward pressure on the head through the mother's lower abdomen. Kirstin nodded for her to begin and lifted the baby upwards, almost as if she was teaching the infant to do a handstand. The baby came to rest on her back on her mother's stomach, with her feet facing towards her mother's head.

As if it were a cork being eased out of a bottle, the head slid free and the newest member of the human race emitted an indignant wail.

Kirstin looked at the infinitely precious little scrap and knew in her heart that her decision had been made.

CHAPTER FOUR

'YES, Kirstin. What can I do for you?' Sam said as he willingly abandoned his pen on top of a stack of papers and leant back in his chair.

With his elbows braced on the arms of the chair he rested his chin on his linked fingers and permitted his eyes just one lightning sweep from the madonna-like purity of her face to her slender feet.

She'd thrown a white coat over her blue scrub suit so she definitely hadn't dressed to impress him. She probably had no idea how faithfully the shapeless drawstring bottoms outlined her long legs and the womanly curve of her hips. When she sat down in front of him and crossed one knee over the other it was done without a second thought for the man opposite her.

His response was utterly predictable and he was glad that he was sitting behind the desk. The last thing he wanted was for her to think he was some sort of pervert.

'Hal spoke to me a couple of hours ago, to ask me if I'd be willing to speak to Sahru Ismail,' she began, and when she'd detailed the arrangements she'd made he was finally able to switch his brain into work mode.

'I think you did the right thing,' he said with an approving nod. 'For women of some ethnic groups, the prospect of being examined by a man must still be difficult, even for someone like Sahru who's working all day with doctors in a hospital.'

He reached for the diary sitting on top of yet another pile of reports awaiting attention. It would take a bit of juggling, with all the work he already had lined up for the next day, but it would be well worth squeezing it in.

'I gather from your tone that you think Sahru might get cold feet if she has to wait to see me. Would it help if you were able to tell her that she can get it all over with at the same time?' he suggested. 'I'll be in the unit at that time, anyway, so if you think Sahru's condition warrants it, and she agrees to let me examine her, all you'd have to do is give me a buzz and I'll come straight in. Then I could give her some sort of an answer straight away.'

'That would be fantastic,' she exclaimed, smiling wholeheartedly this time and sending his pulse rate into orbit. 'I'm certain that Hal would be relieved. I get the feeling that it's taken him a long time to get her to this point and he's on pins, hoping she's not going to change her mind.'

'I take it he's not motivated by pure altruism, then,' Sam commented wryly, and was rewarded by one of Kirstin's more mischievous grins.

'Not at all,' she said with a shake of her head and he watched the way several fugitive coppery strands tried to curl their way inside the flat V of her scrub-suit top. 'He told me in words of one syllable that he was in love with her,' she continued, dragging his mind away from the pale skin of her throat and back to their conversation.

'Don't tell me there's another hospital romance in the offing,' he mocked lightly. 'It's starting to get like one of those over-the-top hospital soaps the patients watch on television. Still, I suppose it's good for our department because they all seem to end up here about nine months later. At least this way we'll never run out of customers.'

She laughed again, but this time she seemed slightly edgy and he hoped she hadn't taken his comment as a dig at her two friends. He certainly hadn't intended it that way...but, then, with his record with women was it surprising that he managed to put his foot in it?

Still, the cause of that was also the cure. His preoccupation with work meant that he had no time to develop the smooth social skills his peers possessed, but he could always bury himself in his work to hide the fact that he didn't have any social skills.

'Was that all?' he asked. He knew he sounded rather abrupt, but he had no idea how to talk to beautiful women if he wasn't discussing their obstetric or gynaecological histories.

'Actually, there was something...' She broke off to sink white teeth into her lower lip, and all he could think about was doing the same.

'Yes?' He drew in a deep breath for control and forced himself to focus on her eyes, but that wasn't much better. They were such a fascinating mixture of colours that they seemed to change from minute to minute. How was he supposed to stop himself wondering what colour they were when she was making love?

'Actually, there's... It's...' Kirstin began, with that slightly shy smile which had captivated him the first time he'd seen it. He doubted that she was aware that her hands were clenched into tight fists inside the pockets of her white coat, but he'd noticed.

Sometimes he thought he noticed every little thing about her, from the stunning colour of her hair and the changeable greeny-hazel of her eyes to the slender elegance of her body. But most of all it was the dedicated woman who lived inside the beautiful body who had captured his interest and come close to stealing his heart.

Not that he could afford to let that happen. There were too many reasons why there could be no future in it for either of them.

For a start, there was the fact that she was a young vibrant woman who, although she was just starting out in her career, was bright enough and determined enough to really make her mark. The future in front of her was far too bright for him to contemplate tying her down—it would be like pulling the wings off a butterfly, or at least, pinning it to a board just so that he could say he possessed it.

'Will you help me have a baby?' she blurted suddenly, urgently, and a tide of colour surged up her pale throat and into her cheeks.

Sam froze in disbelief.

He almost had to remind himself to continue breathing as her words seemed to echo around his consulting room.

Had she really said what he'd just heard? It had sounded like the soundtrack to his wildest dreams—beautiful Titian-haired Kirstin Whittaker asking him to make her pregnant.

Only she didn't know how often she'd starred in those dreams and he'd been very careful that she had no idea how much he'd wanted to bring them to life.

'Would I...what?' he croaked huskily, and had to clear his throat.

It sounded as if he'd swallowed his tongue but at least that was better than tripping over it while his imagination ran riot. He wasn't some hormone-led adolescent, for heaven's sake, he was a thirty-five-year-old man. While he knew from intermittent gossip around the department that Kirstin lived alone, that didn't mean there wasn't a man in her life. There was no excuse for leaping to the conclusion that she was asking *him* to give her a baby. His body was certainly ready, willing and able but that *couldn't* be what she wanted.

Or could it?

Kirstin took one look at the expression on Sam's face and wondered exactly how much of a blunder she'd just made. He looked thunderstruck! Horrified!

'I...I'm sorry if you think I'm taking unfair advantage of my position in the department,' she said hurriedly, frantically trying find the elusive words that would make everything right again. 'I know I should have a letter of referral, but... It's just that...well... it's a very private decision and I know your clerical staff are very discreet but I didn't want to risk drawing adverse attention to the department if it did leak out, and, well, I know that you're not one to allow it to become fodder for the gossip mill...'

'Kirstin?' he said. Just her name.

'Yes,' she whispered, embarrassment making her feel sick. She knew that her face must be glowing because she could feel the heat enveloping her.

'Slow down and take a breath or you'll pass out,' he advised with just a hint of a smile.

That was even worse.

Was he laughing at the absolute ass she'd just made of herself? Or was it the request itself that he found laughable? Unfortunately, even after the months she'd been part of his team, albeit a junior part with much to learn, she didn't know him well enough to tell.

She took his advice and drew a steadying breath, but she was still grateful when he took up the conversation first.

'How about starting again?' he suggested, obviously still fighting the urge to smile as he leant forward to plant both elbows on his desk. 'Only this time can I have the sentences one at a time, in a logical order?'

'Yes. I'm sorry,' she murmured, concentrating on her hands knotted together in her lap. For just a moment she found herself heartily wishing that she'd never embarked on this, but, then, how many options did she have if she wanted a child of her own?

'So you've decided you need help to get pregnant,' he prompted, that dark eyebrow quirking up towards equally dark hair. 'Have you been trying for long? Have you had any tests to determine why you aren't conceiving?'

'No!' Kirstin nearly choked and her cheeks felt as if they were about to burst into flames. 'No, I...I haven't been trying at all. I mean...I'm not in a relationship with anyone.' Nor ever have been, she added silently. That would have meant dropping the barriers, and without them she would be too vulnerable.

'So...don't you think you might be putting the cart before the horse? Wouldn't it be a good idea to find the partner first, then decide to get pregnant?'

'But I don't want a partner!' she exclaimed. 'I have no intention of getting married...*ever*! I want to have a baby and raise him or her myself. When I've completed my time as your registrar, I'll have all the financial security I need, and with Cassie and Naomi around I'll have the emotional support. But most of all I need this for me.'

His brows had drawn together into a swift frown while she was speaking and her heart sank. With the number of childless couples in the area for whom male infertility was the cause, she knew that it was very unusual for hospital funding to even be considered for donor insemination for a single woman. The department could only deal with so many patients at a time and, because of the stringent methods of preparing the donated sperm, the success rates for the process were rarely higher than ten per cent.

She felt even less comfortable with the alternatives. With fewer than a thousand babies available nationally for adoption each year and so many truly infertile couples wanting them, it wouldn't be right for her to apply when there was no reason to suppose that she couldn't carry her own.

'How old are you, Kirstin?' he asked gently.

'Twenty-seven, so I'm certainly old enough to know my own mind,' she pointed out sharply.

'You're also young enough to change your mind about marriage and *still* have time to conceive normally, so why this sudden decision to ask for DI? Have you got a health problem you haven't mentioned? Endometriosis? Early onset menopause? Genetically linked family history of breast cancer? What?'

'No, no. There's nothing like that. I'm completely healthy, as far as I know. And I also know that I won't be changing my mind,' she added stubbornly.

He was silent for a long time, his dark eyes gazing intently at her as if he wanted to be able to get inside her head. Suddenly, he raked the fingers of both hands through his hair and she had the feeling that he'd narrowly prevented himself from pulling it.

'You're crazy!' he exclaimed, and threw himself back in his chair to glare at her from its depths. 'You're young, attractive, intelligent, and you've got your feet planted firmly on a ladder that could take you all the way to the top. If you'd fallen madly in love, like your two friends, I could understand you wanting to start a family now. But to want to do it this way...' He shook his head.

You're young, attractive, intelligent... She replayed the words in her head then totally dismissed the implied compliment as her temper started to simmer.

'Excuse me, Mr Dysart, but I didn't come here to be patronised,' she snapped. 'I'm not some bimbo wanting an instant child as a fashion accessory so I can get my name in the papers. I'm an ordinary woman, working hard to learn an extremely worthwhile job. Please, give me credit for having thought very hard before I came to you for your professional help. With all the things I see every day, it isn't something I'd undertake lightly.'

She drew in a shuddering breath and continued swiftly. 'I could just as easily have opted for a one-night stand—or even a series of one-night stands if the first delivery of three hundred million sperm didn't get me pregnant. Instead, knowing all about the other risks involved in such promiscuous behaviour, I opted to pursue the responsible alternative.'

She was so agitated that she couldn't possibly sit

still any longer, but once she was on her feet it was as if they were cemented to the functional grey carpet.

She stood there in front of his desk and glared across it at him as she fired her final salvo.

'If you would rather I went for Plan A, Mr Dysart, just tell me and I won't waste any more of your time.'

She glared at him, her blood pounding through her veins and her breathing at least twice as fast as it should have been. It was so unfair that he'd been able to trigger such a heated outburst. He certainly wasn't going to feel inclined to help her now.

She didn't know whether she wanted to scream or cry, but using her fists on the wretched man would feel very satisfying right now. Then, when he turned her down, at least she'd have the satisfaction of knowing that she'd...

'I take it you're a natural redhead, then,' he said mildly, and she felt her jaw drop.

She'd half expected him to ask her, very politely, to leave his consulting room—he could be icily polite when the occasion demanded. Yet here he was actually trying to defuse the situation by making a joke linking the colour of her hair to her temper!

Kirstin took a long, slow breath while she calmed down. She took an equally long look at Sam and found herself wondering what made the man tick.

He rarely revealed anything voluntarily but, now that she thought about it, she *had* learned a lot about him since she'd become his registrar.

He was undoubtedly a very dedicated man, spending endless hours at the hospital. He was patience itself when it came to one of his problem patients, infinitely encouraging without ever promising something he knew he couldn't guarantee. He was almost frighteningly intelligent but he certainly wasn't one for blinding people with science in spite of all his qualifications.

As for his looks, she mused as she allowed her eyes to linger on the lean planes of his face, the dark intelligence of his eyes and the unexpected fullness of his mouth. It wasn't that he was male-model beautiful—that type had never appealed to her—but there was something in the symmetry of his features and the impression of power which they emanated that pulled at her emotions like a magnet.

It helped that he had a sense of humour, too. She'd noticed several times that, unlike many men, he could actually laugh at himself. There was a lean elegance about him that was pleasing to the eye, a quiet confidence that carried over into the way he worked.

And yet...

And yet he was so reserved as to be almost secretive. As if there were whole areas of himself and his life to which he allowed no one easy admittance.

'So, if you were to be accepted for DI, what sort of match would you be looking for?' he asked suddenly, startling her out of her thoughts.

She blinked, and it took several seconds for her to realise what he was talking about. While she'd been admiring the man he'd been thinking about her request. Then her spirits rose like a helium-filled balloon. It actually sounded as if he was *seriously* thinking about it!

'As you know, we usually try to match the physical characteristics of the donor with the husband or partner, but in your case...' He shook his head. 'I don't think we've got many donors with your colouring.'

As he looked at her it almost seemed as if the expression in his eyes was one of admiration, and she became aware of a strange sensation deep inside. It felt as if something were unfurling, perhaps a tiny shoot which had been kept in the cold and the dark. With a strange sense of recognition Kirstin suddenly realised that, ordinary as she was, he might be just as attracted to her as she had become towards him.

The revelation completely robbed her of speech. She was barely capable of following what the man was saying as she revelled in the concept of mutual attraction for the first time.

'So, if we were to assume that you *were* acceptable for the donor insemination programme,' he continued, as ever careful not to commit himself or the department irrevocably before he'd established all the information, 'had you had any thoughts as to the physical and mental characteristics of the donor?'

For one crazy second Kirstin thought she was going to laugh aloud. It sounded almost as if he were a car salesman asking her for her preference in paint colours.

'What?' he demanded, and she cursed silently. She should have known that he would pick up on what she was thinking. He didn't seem to miss a thing. 'Something struck you as funny?' He was also persistent enough to keep on asking until she told him what he wanted to know.

'I was just thinking…when you asked me about the donor's physical and mental characteristics…it sounded almost as if you wanted me to decide on the model and colour for a new car,' she admitted wryly.

'Except you wouldn't have the option of trading this one in if you changed your mind later,' Sam pointed out sombrely, continuing the analogy. 'And they usually last a lot longer than a car.'

There was no point in taking umbrage at the way he was spelling everything out in words of one syllable. It was an important part of the process, to weed out the candidates who were unsuitable because their motives were skewed.

In St Augustine's unit, this usually involved several interviews, including one with the psychologist. Was Sam going to undertake that as well? It would certainly limit the number of people who would be in on her secret.

She was sitting looking at him as he tapped his steepled index fingers against his lips, his dark eyes fixed intently on her with a thoughtful frown on his face before he began to speak again.

'So, *have* you made any sort of decision about who you'd want to father your child?' he asked, returning to the question she'd never answered. 'Obviously, you know that all the donors are anonymous, but what sort of person do you want him to be?'

This was one part of the process that she'd worried about—what traits she wanted joined with hers to make her child. Knowing that she never intended marrying, she'd never sighed after the boys at school. There had been no particular type of man who'd set her pulse racing, until...

Kirstin stared across at him, her eyes fixed on the face of the only man she'd ever been aware of while her thoughts slowly stopped their dizzying whirl. With a strange sense of inevitability she looked deep into his eyes and realised that the only man she wanted to father her child was Sam Dysart.

'Kirstin?' he prompted when she stared silently at him wondering where to go from here.

'I…ah…well…' she fumbled, mutely cursing the pale skin that, even now, was flushing bright red again.

'What about basic things? Height and build, for example,' he proposed helpfully.

She grabbed at the suggestion gratefully, knowing she would never be able to have what she really wanted.

'About your height and build,' she began, and had to suppress a smile when he reacted as though stung. She hadn't expected him to be self-conscious.

'Ah, are you sure?' he said, looking distinctly uncomfortable as he picked up his pen and pretended to make a note. He certainly couldn't meet her eyes.

'Absolutely,' she said quietly, deciding there and then to sound him out. If he *was* attracted to her, perhaps there would be a chance…

At least she'd get to tell him, in an indirect way, what she liked about him. 'You're tall without being too lanky and ungainly, and your build is athletic without being bulky and over-developed.'

Somehow he managed to keep his poker face, but his hand tightened around his pen until she thought it would snap and she actually heard him swallow hard. Oh, it was nice in a totally unexpected way to know that her words were having an effect on him. She'd cut herself off from the whole dating scene so thoroughly that she'd never realised that this man-woman thing could actually be fun.

'What colouring?' he said doggedly, but even those few syllables told her his voice had grown huskier.

'Brown,' she said decisively, becoming more convinced with every second she spent thinking about it. 'Dark brown hair, with a bit of natural curl to it, and dark brown eyes. Big, serious dark brown eyes that shine when he laughs.'

He grew very still and for a long moment, while she waited to see what he would do, Kirstin wondered if she'd gone too far.

But what *was* too far? She admired the man, physically and mentally. How could anything she said be too far when what she really wanted to say was, Sam, I want *you* to give me your baby?

In the blink of an eye she could see her child in those first few minutes of life, his big dark eyes wide open and gazing up at her. He'd have a peach fuzz layer of silky dark hair over his head and his long fingers would be a miniature version of his father's.

Later, when he took his tentative first steps, there would be determination in his total concentration, as there would be when he learned to kick his first football and ride his first bike.

All too clearly she could see what he would look like when he began to grow taller, his legs coltish until he learned to control them with the same elegance as his father.

Other details were hazier.

Would he have the same thoughtful way of speaking and would he inherit the same way of raising one eyebrow that Sam had, or was it something that he could only pick up by imitation? If she and Sam were still working at St Augustine's, she might even have occasion to see the two of them together at some social function…

If only it could come true, but it was all just a dream.

Finally Sam raised his very serious dark brown eyes to meet hers and his expression was a forbidding mixture of anger and pain.

'This isn't a game, Kirstin,' he said ominously, and something inside her quivered in an echo of the pain she'd caused him.

'We're talking about the man you want to father a child for you,' he continued inexorably. 'And I'm trying to establish what sort of physical characteristics you'd like him to have.'

'And I'm telling you,' she said equally seriously, suddenly knowing that she'd reached the point of no return. She had to say something now, or she'd always wonder what might have happened if only...

'I promise you, I'm not treating any of this as a game,' she said softly. Her lips were dry with nerves and she had to moisten them with her tongue before she could continue. 'The physical and mental characteristics I'd like my baby's father to have are the same as yours because I'd like *you* to be the father.'

The words were still vibrating in the air between them when, with the worst of all possible timing, both her pager and his phone began to shrill imperatively.

Even though she had to reach blindly for the pocket of her white coat to find the noisy contraption, she couldn't look away from him. And the way he fumbled for the receiver told her that his concentration was similarly absorbed.

'Yes?' he growled, his eyes full of roiling emotion that circumstances wouldn't allow him to voice. 'Sam Dysart.'

The expression on Sam's face as he listened to the rapid-fire voice on the other end and asked his own questions told Kirstin that she wouldn't need to make her own call. Whatever it was, it was urgent enough for the message to go out to anyone and everyone within reach.

'How high is her blood pressure? Is she retaining fluids? Any protein in her urine?' he demanded urgently, barely waiting to hear the reply before he fired the next question.

'Right, get four grams of magnesium sulphate into her, and if you haven't got the magnesium to hand, make it diazepam, ten milligrams. Fast! Then get her up to Theatre. Have you got hold of Dr Halawa? Dr Whittaker is with me. We're on our way now, and we'll bring some magnesium with us in case you haven't got any,' he promised, and virtually threw the receiver back in position.

'Pre-eclampsia?' Kirstin guessed, already out of her seat and making for the door.

'Worse. It's fulminating pre-eclampsia,' he said grimly, his long legs getting him there that much faster. 'Her blood pressure's sky high and she's got enormous amounts of protein in her urine. She's already fitting, she's in premature labour and apparently it's a totally impossible footling presentation.'

They took off along the corridor and Kirstin wondered if their patient would have a fatal stroke before they even reached her. It was a serious risk when blood pressure rose so high so fast. And the chances that the baby could survive such a condition were slim to none, even without the dangers of prematurity.

'This is my first,' she admitted as Sam shouldered open the door to the stairwell.

'Fulminating pre-eclampsia or footling?' he queried over his shoulder as he took the stairs two at a time.

'Both.' She was having to run to keep up with him and he wasn't even breathing heavily. 'Antenatal usually picks up the pre-eclampsia before it can progress too far, and I've only seen footling presentations in the textbooks.'

He wrenched the door open at the top of the stairs, holding it until she was safely through before taking off again along the corridor.

'Well, it doesn't sound as if this one is going to be anything other than an emergency Caesarean if we're going to save the mother. I've no idea yet what gestational age we've got for the baby.'

His tie was already undone and draped down either side of his chest and one hand was already slipping buttons open down the front of his shirt as he made for the changing room.

Over the scrub sinks they met just long enough for him to pass on the most recent information on their patient's condition and then they were donning masks and gloves.

'She's stopped fitting,' Hal reported as they arrived beside their unconscious patient, 'but the magnesium is depressing her breathing. She's only on twelve per minute and her kidneys are packing up.'

'Is someone keeping a check on her patellar reflex?' Sam demanded while he waited for the operating area to be prepped and draped, reminding Kirstin that the reflex would disappear if the concentration of magnesium became dangerously high.

If she hadn't known about the urgency of the operation, Kirstin wouldn't have been able to tell from Sam's behaviour. Outwardly, he seemed as calm and methodical as ever, but she could sense an extra intensity to his deliberation as he made the initial incision.

Kirstin was on her mettle, needing no verbal instruction to tell her to clear the operating field of blood as soon as possible.

The whole operation was similar to dozens she'd seen him perform since she'd started work with the team, but this time it seemed almost to be happening at twice the speed.

It was apparently just seconds after that first incision that he was reaching carefully into the gaping wound to begin to retrieve the fragile creature trapped within.

'Thirty-four weeks at most,' he guessed as he gestured for Kirstin to support his tiny burden while he untangled the limbs from the umbilicus and drew the dangling foot back up through the cervix. 'Is everything ready for me to cut the umbilicus? Oxygen?'

'All ready,' Luke Thornton confirmed as he stood by ready to hurry his latest charge to the special care baby unit. 'How's he looking?'

'He's a she,' Sam said with a trace of a smile in his voice, 'so she might just have a little bit better chance of surviving, but I'll leave that to you. How's Mrs Frazer doing?' The operation wasn't even half-over yet, with the placenta still to separate and the wound to suture, and Sam's concentration had obviously returned to its single track.

As soon as the job was over, the unconscious woman would have to be transferred straight to Intensive Care as she would need constant one-to-one care not available on Obs and Gyn.

If the amount of magnesium in her system dropped too low, she could begin fitting again, while if it went too high her breathing would be compromised. It would be a very complicated balancing act until her body began to recover from the demands made on it by its recently terminated pregnancy.

There was the inevitable sense of anticlimax when the trolley was wheeled through to Post-Op and everyone dispersed.

Kirstin climbed into the shower and stood for several minutes with the hot water pouring down on the back of her neck, uncaring that her hair might be getting wet.

Of course, she was relieved that both mother and daughter had survived, but now all she could think about was the conversation the emergency had interrupted. She drew in a deep breath and held it, fighting the tears that were threatening to fall.

Why had it taken her so long to realise that it wasn't just *any* baby she wanted but *Sam's* baby? If she'd recognised it sooner, would she have been able to put her case more clearly, more persuasively?

It was so frustrating that once they'd left his room Sam hadn't had a chance to refer to their conversation.

What had he been thinking when the phone had rung and would she ever know?

Had he been flattered? Appalled? Intrigued? All of them? None of them?

He hadn't been too receptive to the idea of her wanting DI in the first place, but he'd slowly seemed to be softening towards it as their meeting had continued.

Her realisation that she wouldn't be satisfied with anything other than *his* child had stunned her. She honestly hadn't known until that moment exactly how strong her feelings had grown, and there had been no time to come to terms with them before she'd opened her mouth to voice her request.

Kirstin reached for a towel and pressed it against her face while she tried to remember the words to every prayer she'd ever learned.

Her biggest fear now was that the discussion had ended at such a crucial point. If she'd had the chance to explain her reasons, he might be more understanding. As it was, he was probably going to wipe his hands of her completely.

CHAPTER FIVE

'I WAS beginning to think you'd drowned,' said a gruff voice when Kirstin finally emerged into the corridor.

'Sam,' she breathed, half in dismay and half in pleasure. The last thing she'd expected had been to find him out here, leaning nonchalantly against the wall and obviously waiting for her. His well-worn jeans and thick jumper topped by damp hair still bearing the marks of his comb were witness to the fact that he'd showered, too.

'I thought you would have gone home ages ago,' she said, not certain whether that had been wishful thinking. Now that the confrontation was at hand she found herself turning into a coward.

'I've just been into Intensive Care, checking up on Mrs Frazer.' He gestured towards the corridor behind him.

'How's she doing?' The poor woman had still looked dreadful as she'd been wheeled out at the end of the emergency surgery, so swollen that her features had barely been recognisable. It was easy to see that she'd just come desperately close to dying.

'Her kidney function is picking up a bit but her blood pressure's going to take a lot longer to stabilise. We won't know how much permanent damage has been done for some time yet.

'In the meantime, her daughter is doing better than anyone expected. She weighed in at just three pounds four ounces and, even though it's only an hour since she was born, she's already out of the incubator and off oxygen. It looks like she's turning out to be a real little fighter,' he reported with a brief smile. 'Hal's on duty tonight, so he'll keep an eye on both of them. Anyway, I'll have my pager switched on in case I'm needed.'

In the midst of Kirstin's chaotic thoughts, one emerged quite clearly. It was so typical of Sam to volunteer to come in, even though he was officially off duty. He had a real sense of commitment, not just to his job but also to each individual patient.

'Well, I'd better go,' she said into the uneasy silence, suddenly dreading hearing him say the final no that would spell the end of her dream. She hadn't realised that it could mean so much to her...

'We need to talk,' he said abruptly. He didn't attempt to touch her but the quiet words stopped her in her tracks as effectively as if he'd physically restrained her.

It was hardly surprising that their thoughts should be circling the same topic, but she hadn't expected to hear the pain in his voice.

'I have to be here early tomorrow to see Sahru,' Kirstin said weakly, wondering when she'd become such a coward.

'So do I,' Sam reminded her with a distinctly sharp edge to his voice. 'But this won't wait. Where do you want to go? Back to my office?'

'Not here.' She shook her head firmly and glanced from side to side. Their conversation was inevitable but on hospital premises there was far too much likelihood that someone would see the two of them together off duty and wonder what was going on. 'The hospital grapevine isn't particularly noted for checking the facts of a story before the embellishments start.'

He snorted. 'You don't have to tell me. Remember, just after you started your registrarship, those two nurses who arrived on duty drenched to the skin from a sudden downpour?'

'And within minutes, the story going the rounds was that the two of them had been caught together in the shower,' Kirstin finished. 'Yes, I remember.'

'So, where to? Neither of us has had a chance to eat so we could go out for a meal. Or would you prefer to go home?'

Home? The word always made her ache a little even at her age.

Apart from those three life-altering years with Dot, she'd never really known what a real home was supposed to be. She'd been orphaned too young to have any clear memories, just shadowy impressions of a lady who was surrounded by the scent of lavender.

Her own little bolthole was nothing more than a refuge from the world and only Cassie and Naomi had ever been invited to visit.

She glanced down at her disreputable jeans with a grimace. 'I don't think I'd like to go anywhere that would accept me looking like this,' she said wryly.

'How about coming home with me if I promise to feed you? I'll also promise to give you a lift home when we've finished.'

There was a brief spurt of pleasure at the thought of Sam Dysart, consultant gynaecologist and obstetrician, cooking a meal for her but all she could think were the ominous words, 'The condemned woman ate a hearty meal…'

'Kirstin?' he prompted, and she nodded, resigned to getting everything over and done with as soon as possible.

They always said it minimised the pain to make the cut swift and clean, but did that also apply when it was the death of a dream?

'Take your coat off,' Sam invited as he ushered Kirstin through the front door. 'I've just got to make a quick phone call.'

He strode off down the hallway, lobbing his jacket over the newel post at the end of the stairs on his way past, and silence closed in around her.

'What am I doing here?' she muttered as she unzipped her padded jacket. She'd never felt so uncomfortable in her life.

Until a few minutes ago, when he'd drawn up in the driveway in his comfortable but nondescript car, she hadn't even known where Sam lived. And now she was here, in his home, to discuss her...her proposition.

Where had her brain been, to have blurted out that she wanted *him* to father her child? Until today, the two of them had only the most marginal of relationships, that of junior and senior in a busy hospital department.

This was an impossible situation and the sooner she got herself out of it, the better. Her flat was only a couple of streets away. It would only take a few seconds to put her jacket back on and then she'd be out of the door and gone. Sam was intelligent enough to realise that she'd changed her mind.

She was still struggling to force one hand into a sleeve that had turned the wrong way when she heard him returning, and knew with a sinking heart that she'd missed her chance.

'Do you want to come through to the kitchen while I make us some coffee? The food will take about fifteen minutes but we'll have to take it through to the sitting room. I'm afraid I turned the dining room into an office just until I get the time to sort out the spare bedroom.'

Kirstin found herself staring at her unflappable boss in disbelief. She'd never seen him like this before, nervously talking and pacing. Suddenly she realised that he was as on edge about having her in his home as she was about being there.

With the realisation came a measure of relief and she was actually able to hold a semi-coherent conversation with him while he made the coffee and took out plates and cutlery.

There was still the meal to get through and a lot of uncomfortable silence to fill, but perhaps they *were* going to be able to have a civilised discussion about her options after all.

Quite apart from the fact that they spent a lot of their time working together, it wouldn't do either of them any harm if they concentrated on learning a bit more about each other. She was certainly willing to take advantage of tonight's opportunity. She'd always found Sam a fascinating man, not least because she sensed some hidden secret in his life.

Anyway, if nothing came of her wish for him to father her child, at least it might mean they would know each other well enough to smooth out any rough patches in their future working relationship.

'That was cheating!' she accused with a chuckle as she carried two warm plates, serving spoons and two pairs of beautifully decorated chopsticks in his wake. 'You said you were going to cook.'

The fifteen minutes he'd promised had turned out to be thirty before there'd been a ring at the door with a special delivery from the Chinese restaurant around the corner.

It had been a strange half-hour, the first few minutes stretching uncomfortably while they'd tentatively introduced the usual topics of conversation in an attempt to find common ground. Then Kirstin had asked Sam if he'd seen the latest paper which apparently confirmed that babies who were put to sleep in darkened rooms ended up with higher IQs than those who slept with nightlights on, and time had simply flown by.

'Actually, I only promised to feed you,' Sam pointed out smugly as he deposited a tray full of foil cartons on the coffee-table in front of the settee. 'And Mr Lau at the Oriental Garden can do this stuff a lot better and faster than I can, especially after an adrenaline job like Mrs Frazer. Come on. Sit down and tuck in.'

He sank onto one end of the solitary settee and immediately reached for a serving spoon, obviously hungry and clearly relaxed enough in her company now not to feel that he had to stand on ceremony.

Mention of the woman's name put a frown on Kirstin's forehead. 'I still don't understand how she got into that state,' she commented as she opted to kneel on the thick rug on the opposite side of the low table and reached for the other plate. 'Where was she going for her antenatal care that they didn't pick up on it?'

'I was wondering about that, too,' Sam mumbled around a mouthful. 'I was working up a good head of steam ready to chew her husband out as soon as he showed his face. I was actually up in Intensive Care with her when he arrived, and the poor man was absolutely distraught.'

He paused just long enough to fight with a messy bundle of bean sprouts before continuing.

'He said that they moved house about a month ago and he's been working a long shift away from home since then so he could have the time off when the baby was due. Apparently, because his wife was so busy setting the house to rights, she must have forgotten all about registering straight away with a new hospital.'

'At thirty-four weeks, she probably thought she still had plenty of time,' Kirstin suggested as she belatedly picked up her chopsticks, heartily glad she was reasonably proficient with them or she might starve to death. She'd been amused that Sam had just assumed that she knew how to use them, his own skill obviously well practised.

'She might have got away with the oversight, except that fulminating pre-eclampsia is particularly vicious and can come on frighteningly fast. Thank God it's relatively rare,' he added around another mouthful of chicken and bamboo shoots.

Kirstin murmured her agreement as she closed her eyes in ecstasy. She was so hungry that she would have been grateful for beans on toast, but this was delicious. Conversation lapsed entirely while they concentrated on clearing their plates, then filled them again.

'More?' he offered, holding out the last of the spe-

cial fried rice and waving his chopsticks over the last
morsels left in the assorted foil containers.

'No! No more!' She leant back on her hands and
groaned. 'I'm going to need a crane to get me up off
the floor as it is!'

'So there's no room for dessert?' he teased as he
began to pile the debris back onto the tray. 'I've got
at least half a gallon of ice cream in the freezer and
it's got chunks of real Belgian chocolate in it.'

'That's not fair!' she wailed. 'If you knew what a
sweet tooth I've got…and I can't eat another thing.'

'Next time you'll have to leave some room,' he
advised, and just like that the atmosphere between
them changed.

Next time? That implied that this wouldn't be her
only visit to his house. Did that mean he'd made his
decision in her favour? It was almost too incredible
to believe and she hardly dared to ask.

'Sam?' Her voice was quivering with nerves and it
was a good job she was sitting down or she would
have fallen.

This meant so much to her. So much more than
she'd ever realised it could.

'Does that mean you're going to do it?' she demanded softly as he straightened up with the laden
tray in his hands.

'Do it?' he asked, frowning as he looked down at
her. She had to crane her head right back to see his
dark eyes but she saw the moment her meaning registered.

For just a split second there was a flare of something that looked almost like fear and then his expression went totally blank. 'Good God, no!' he exclaimed emphatically.

Her heart was shattering even as the tray was un-ceremoniously dumped back on the table.

For just those few precious seconds she'd really believed that he was going to help her to have a child—*his* child—and now it had all been snatched away again.

Before she even realised it was going to happen, tears began to trickle down her cheeks and she covered her face with her hands. She was devastated at his adamant refusal but it had finally brought home to her that she'd made an utter fool of herself.

This was Sam Dysart, her boss. What on earth had given her the idea that he would agree to something so…so outrageous? He didn't know just how much it meant to her.

'Kirstin, no. Don't cry. It's… You don't understand,' he was saying, clearly concerned about her in spite of the embarrassing situation. Even without looking at him she could hear the misery in his voice.

'Of c-course I understand,' she sobbed miserably as she finally had to admit to herself all the reasons it had been impossible from the outset.

'I was a fool to even th-think you'd agree. You're a consultant and I'm your registrar. Some trigger-happy lawyer could probably make a case for sexual misconduct and it could compromise your position at the hospital if it ever got out. And there are probably thirty thousand regulations you would have been breaking, and why would you want someone like me to have your child, anyway? You want to wait until you get married, of course, not have offspring littered about…'

'No, Kirstin. Listen,' he said insistently. 'It's not

like that. I would have loved to help you but...I can't... I won't be having any children...ever.'

When his final word registered in Kirstin's brain she drew in a shocked breath.

Slowly, she pulled her hands away from her face and gazed up and up until she could see his face. He began to turn away as though he didn't want to meet her eyes but then she saw his shoulders stiffen and he turned back to face her.

'Ever?' she repeated in disbelief, her breath catching as she absently smeared the tears away with her fingers. She hardly cared what she looked like. What mattered was this new bombshell that had exploded in front of her.

'But...but, why, Sam?' she asked as she clumsily scrambled to her feet, needing to be upright so she had a better chance of reading his expression. 'You'd be a brilliant father,' she continued passionately. 'I've seen you with the babies and when you call in on the kids in Paediatrics. You should have a dozen at least.'

His face twisted into a parody of a smile. 'A bit excessive, but thank you for the vote of confidence,' he said wearily.

'No, I mean it,' she insisted. 'Why *don't* you want to? I don't understa— Oh, God!' she groaned as the answer suddenly came to her. 'Infertility! That's why you went into this speciality, isn't it? So you could do research into infertility to help men with the same problem as you. Oh, Sam, I'm so sorry for putting my foot into something so private. I'd never have said anything... I will never say anything. No one will ever know...'

'Whoa, Kirstin, whoa! You've got it all wrong,' he said, the wash of colour travelling quickly up his throat and over his cheeks clearly demonstrating just how embarrassed he was.

As if trying to remove the evidence, he rubbed both hands over his face then ran the fingers of both hands roughly through his hair to leave it standing up in every direction. Not at all like the neatly groomed consultant his patients saw.

Kirstin felt like pulling her own hair out. This conversation was getting more convoluted by the minute.

'Well, if I've got everything wrong, how about putting me straight?' she challenged as she fished in her pocket for a rather bedraggled paper hankie. She gave a ferocious blow and stuffed it away again. 'It seems as if every time I open my mouth I put my foot in it.'

Sam hesitated, his eyes apparently fixed on the remains of their recent meal, and for a moment she thought he was going to tell her to mind her own business. Then he shrugged.

'Let me clear this mess away first and bring some coffee in. I'd rather have a large brandy, but if Hal calls…'

Kirstin grimaced at his retreating back. As ever, his consideration for his patients overrode his own needs and as she grabbed the last of the debris from their meal she found herself wondering if the man ever put himself first.

It was fully dark outside now, and the bright fluorescent light threw the meagre decorations of the kitchen into stark prominence. Everything was so basic and so unadorned that the atmosphere was almost arid. Stainless steel and white wherever she looked. Everything spotlessly clean and nothing out of place. It was so bland and blank and needed…something.

Something to make it into a real home, she decided, although quite what that was, she had no idea.

'You could almost perform surgery in here,' she quipped as she grabbed a teatowel, strangely pleased to find that he preferred to get the dirty dishes cleaned up straight away. The attempt at conversation was just a way of breaking what could otherwise be a very uncomfortable silence. 'The sitting room is rather minimalist, too. Is the rest of the house the same?'

Sam looked up from the plate he was cleaning and glanced around, then shrugged. 'I suppose so, pretty much, but without the stainless steel. I hadn't really noticed. I don't spend much time here, except to sleep and—' He broke off at the sound of scratching, listened for a moment and then smiled, the expression reaching right up to his eyes.

'What's that? Is there something outside the back door?'

'Some*one*,' he corrected quietly, and reached for the bowl on the other side of the work surface. Inside it Kirstin could see various leftovers from their meal. 'Will you excuse me while I take care of my other guest?'

He walked across to the door and unlocked it in a strangely furtive way before crouching down.

'Hey, Mac,' he called softly as he eased the door open. He obviously didn't want to frighten whoever was on the other side. 'Nice of you to visit me tonight. Are you going to do me the favour of getting rid of this lot?'

He continued to speak an almost continuous monologue while Kirstin peered carefully over his shoulder to watch a lop-eared, battle-scarred old ginger cat attack the scraps.

'Is he yours?' she breathed softly, the cold air turning her words to vapour that billowed around both their heads before dispersing.

'Oh, no,' Sam said, making the words part of his soothing litany. 'Mac doesn't belong to a mere human. Mac belongs to himself. He just deigns to come visiting every so often and somehow manages to time it just right to help me out with a disposal problem. Of course, I tried feeding him on that ready-made stuff in tins, but you'd have thought I was trying to feed him *cat* food. He completely turned his nose up at it and demanded real *people* food.'

Kirstin smiled as she listened to Sam's nonsense, easing herself to one side so that she could see their visitor more clearly.

She thought she'd been very careful, but there was obviously nothing wrong with the one good eye Mac had left.

He froze, a crouching, wary statue, while his tail lashed angrily from side to side. Kirstin froze, too, not certain what else to do.

'Hey, Mac, what can I tell you?' Sam continued smoothly. 'If I'd known you were going to be here I wouldn't have asked her to visit, but you're a man of the world so you know how it is. Do you want me to introduce you?' He flicked a glance at Kirstin over his shoulder.

'Hey, Mac,' Kirstin said softly, deliberately copying Sam's words as well as his tone. She wasn't happy to see the way all his fur went up right along his back. The last thing she wanted to do was scare him. 'I'm sorry to intrude on your dining arrangements. I can go away if you'd prefer.'

Wary of upsetting him, she kept her eyes firmly

fixed on him as she steadied herself with one hand on the frame of the door, concentrating on moving very slowly.

'Well, I'm damned,' Sam breathed as the cagey creature's head came up and he sniffed delicately in Kirstin's direction. She couldn't believe it either when he straightened up out of his defensive crouch and took a tentative step in her direction.

'Well, old friend, if you don't know the word "traitor", it's about time you learned it,' Sam said wryly. 'I've been feeding you ever since I moved into this house and you've never once let me get within reach. A woman reaches out her hand and...' He was lost for words, as Kirstin was when the scarred old head butted daintily against her hand in a demand for attention.

Tentatively she obliged and was rewarded with a brief rusty purr before the creature decided things had gone far enough. In the space of a couple of seconds he'd withdrawn from the fleeting contact and had disappeared into the shadows of the winter night.

It was only then that Kirstin realised that she was draped over Sam's shoulder like a shawl, one hand still resting on his thigh for support from when she'd reached out towards Mac.

Hastily she scrambled to her feet and took a step back to break all contact between them. The cold March wind replaced the heat of Sam's body against her and made her shiver, but that wasn't what was making her skin so sensitive to the brush of fabric against it.

'He didn't have any water,' she said, hoping she hadn't given herself away. Could Sam tell that she was reacting to the contact between their bodies, that she hadn't wanted to break it?

'I'll put some out in a while in case he comes back later,' he said as he closed the door.

For some reason the click of the lock seemed almost unbearably intimate, audible evidence that the two of them were enclosed in the house together.

'I'll bring the coffee through,' he offered. 'You go and make yourself comfortable.'

His voice sounded so calm that Kirstin wondered how he'd managed to get himself on an even keel so quickly. She was going to need more than a minute or two to get her own emotions under control, otherwise she was liable to make a complete fool of herself all over again.

I never cry, she reminded herself fiercely as she stood in the middle of the stark sitting room. I am calm and in control and I will not make this situation any worse for him than it is already.

She glanced from the slightly shabby reclining chair on one side of the fireplace to the settee Sam had sat on to eat his meal. For her own peace of mind she would rather sit in the chair, but it was a ridiculously long way away from the settee and it would make it look as if she was afraid to be too near him.

She strode across to the settee and dropped into one corner, placing her linked fingers neatly in her lap while she waited for Sam. She'd spent years perfecting her poker face, and now would be a very good time for her to use it.

Apart from hiding her own disappointment, it was also important that she shouldn't make it any harder for Sam to reveal his confidences.

'As you're off duty, I made yours with warm milk

and a touch of sugar,' he said, startling her out of her thoughts. 'That *is* right, isn't it?'

Kirstin blinked. 'At this time of night, yes,' she confirmed, bemused that he'd noticed such an unimportant thing. When she was going to be in Theatre, she didn't drink coffee at all, and during the day she took whatever she could get her hands on to keep her motors firing, but that last cup at the end of each shift was her own little indulgence taken purely for pleasure and comfort.

She reached out to take the mug from him, careful not to allow their hands to touch, or their bodies when he settled in the opposite corner of the settee. She needed all her wits about her now.

Kirstin had expected him to start speaking once he'd settled but he seemed far too interested in watching the steam rising from the liquid in his own mug.

There was only so long that she could let the silence draw out before the tension got to her.

'Why aren't you married?' she blurted, the words emerging before she could put a stop to them. Every so often she was sure she caught glimpses of pain and sorrow behind the calm professional exterior. 'You said you came close, once,' she persisted, wondering where she got her nerve.

'Never married. Never divorced,' Sam returned simply.

'Never come close?' she persisted, wondering where she got the nerve. Her intuition was telling her that she might be on the right track. There was something in the way his shoulders had stiffened and his hand had tightened around his mug of coffee. There was also the fact that he wouldn't meet her eyes. Still, if he didn't want to answer, he didn't have to.

From the way the silence lengthened between them she thought he'd decided it was none of her business, until he suddenly looked up at her and she was caught in the blaze of his gaze like a doe transfixed by head-lights.

The expression in his eyes was so filled with sorrow and an unnamed despair that it was almost as if a hand tightened itself around her heart.

'Yes, I came close, once,' he said in a raw voice, his eyes once more fixed on the mug now clasped between both hands like some sort of lifeline. 'At least, I thought we were until…' He paused and she held her breath, afraid to make a sound in case he stopped. Then, almost as if he'd come to a decision, he met her gaze again and this time his expression was fierce, almost challenging.

'Until I told her that I'm severely dyslexic,' he continued with a touch of defiance. 'Also, that some studies have shown a pattern of genetic inheritance of the condition.'

'And?' she prompted with a frown. 'Dyslexia's a problem but hardly a life-threatening one and certainly nothing to be ashamed of. And, anyway, I've certainly never noticed any evidence of it in your work.'

He gave a single harsh bark of laughter. 'Ah, Kirstin Whittaker, what a pity I didn't know you then. I could have asked you to have a word with Lissa when she turned me and my flawed genes down. You could have told her there was nothing to worry about.'

'Honestly, Sam. If you hadn't told me, I'd never have known,' she protested, hating to hear that thread of bitterness in his voice. Her brain was busy dissecting the many hours they'd spent together over the last few weeks and months. Now that she knew what she was looking for, a pattern was beginning to emerge.

'That's why you always dictate your instructions about treatment and drugs, isn't it?' she asked with a smile of revelation. It was a cleverly devised system, bearing in mind the danger that he could transpose letters and numbers, or even leave some out entirely. 'And you always take armfuls of stuff home with you to go over in your own time, so you won't miss anything by trying to rush through it during your shift.'

It was little more than thinking aloud, so there was no need for him to comment, but the more she thought about it the more amazed she was by what Sam had achieved in spite of his problem. He must be spending endless hours going over every little detail just to make sure he didn't let one of his patients down.

'How severely are you affected? How long does it take you to read a journal?' she demanded suddenly, then shook her head. 'No. Don't tell me, or you'll have me feeling guilty about the fact that I can speed-read. Good God, Sam, did the woman realise what she was giving up? A man of your intelligence, with the determination to keep working until he succeeds, no matter what the odds, no matter how long it takes. And you've got *how* many qualifications so far?'

She shook her head at the mind-boggling number of hours he must have spent studying to pass so many exams, and her opinion of him grew beyond bounds.

'Oh, Sam,' she said softly, feeling almost overwhelmed by the mixture of emotions flooding through her. 'Intelligence, determination, persistence, dedication, a caring nature…what a wonderful genetic inheritance to pass on to a child.'

'A child who inherits dyslexia might not agree,' he said darkly, and she could only imagine the torment his childhood must have been. Had he been one of the children who had been pilloried as stupid when all he'd needed had been help to direct his efforts?

'But the education system has changed, and if he had a father who had conquered it and gone on to make a success of his life in spite of the dyslexia…' She knew she sounded as if she was begging him to change his mind but she didn't care.

The woman he'd loved might have viewed it as an insuperable problem but as far as she was concerned Sam, the whole man, was more important.

Kirstin watched the expressions chasing each other across his face and her heart began to melt. It was obvious that he was trying to come to terms with the fact that knowing about his disability hadn't changed her mind.

She'd never realised what a can of worms she'd be opening when she'd first approached her superior about applying for DI. Neither had she realised that it would open her eyes to him as a man.

In fact, the more she found out about him, the more she was coming to realise that he was someone she could actually fall in love with.

CHAPTER SIX

'SAHRU, come in,' Kirstin said with a welcoming smile and gestured towards the chairs on either side of a small coffee-table.

It was difficult in such small rooms to achieve the right ambience for patients to feel relaxed enough to let down their protective shields. At least the upholstered armchairs she'd grouped in this corner were better than the institutional stacking chairs that used to sit in front of the desk.

'I should not be wasting your time like this,' the beautiful young woman protested as she nervously sank into the furthest seat. 'You have so many women who want to have children, while I—' She broke off to shake her head but Kirstin had already seen the sad expression in her dark eyes.

Kristin cared deeply about all her patients, but suddenly she was gripped with a strange sense of urgency about this woman and her difficulties.

'Why don't you tell me about your problem and then we can decide whether you're wasting my time,' she suggested softly. 'Do I understand that you were brought up in a very...traditional family in Sudan?'

Sahru was obviously an intelligent woman and Kirstin knew from the quick quirk of one corner of her mouth that she appreciated the euphemistic way the topic had been broached.

'Very traditional,' she confirmed expressionlessly. 'I was...*operated* on when I was five years old.'

Five? Kirstin barely suppressed a gasp. 'And you've had problems ever since?'

'I nearly died,' she said softly, and Kirstin saw her eyes filling with shadows as she looked inward towards the remembered horror. 'First when the bleeding would not stop, and then from an infection... I have had many infections.'

Kirstin had difficulty subduing a shudder but this wasn't about her reactions, it was about Sahru's disfigurement and its continuing effect on her health.

'So what problems has it left you with?' Kirstin prompted, concentrating on the here and now. 'Is it just problems each month or do you also have difficulty passing water?'

'Both,' Sahru said succinctly. 'The aperture is too small and it creates too much pressure and that makes pain.' She shrugged fatalistically. 'Each month I must have days away from my work because I cannot stand upright. Every day I must watch how much I drink because it takes so long to urinate.'

Kirstin could hardly imagine what it must be like to have to plan every day and every month so carefully. She was lucky enough to be able to take her bodily functions for granted. What must it be like...?

Hastily, she reined in her thoughts. This was neither the time nor the place for empathising except in a helpful way.

'Will you let me examine you, Sahru?' she asked. 'To see how bad the problem is?'

'Is all this really necessary?' Sahru asked uncertainly, clearly uncomfortable with the idea. 'I will not be having children, so there is no real need for anything to change...down there. It does not need to be made more open for a man to...'

She ran out of words, but Kirstin knew only too well what she was saying. Her search on the Internet had yielded more details about such things than had been comfortable.

'This isn't about doing something for the approval of a man, or to deliberately go against one,' she said gently. 'I know that to undo at least part of what was done when you were five would be against everything you were taught. But this isn't about Hal, or your family or your traditions—it's about your health and doing something just for *you*. To see if there is something that can be done to make your days more comfortable, your life more bearable.'

Sahru was apprehensive—that was easy to see in the tension vibrating through her. Kirstin ached to be able to say something that would ease the mental anguish she must be going through. It must be so hard to go against a lifetime of believing that the injuries inflicted on her had been for her own good.

'Be brave, Sahru,' Kirstin murmured encouragingly, reaching out to touch the tightly knotted hands. 'You've already travelled a long way from your country to find a different life… Now do something to make that life more pleasant.'

The silence didn't last much longer.

'You are right,' the young woman said with a lift of her chin as she stood up tall and strong. 'It *is* time.'

Kirstin showed her through to the adjoining examining room and gave her some privacy to slip out of her uniform and into a gown.

Back at her desk she reached for the phone and suddenly realised that her hand was trembling. Irritated, she drew in a steadying breath and tapped the numbers out with more force than was strictly necessary.

'Sam Dysart,' said the deep voice in her ear, and her throat closed up as something deep inside her burst into life.

When had just the sound of his voice had this effect on her? she thought, her panicked thoughts whirling around in her head. Was it a result of their inconclusive conversation last night?

Before he'd fulfilled his promise to take her home he'd sat in silence for some time, his mind turned inward while he'd followed his own thoughts.

She'd waited with bated breath, but when he'd finally looked at her she'd known he hadn't been ready to make a decision.

'I need time to think, Kirstin,' he'd said, and her heart had sunk. Much as she'd have liked to have forced the issue she'd had to respect his wishes, but, oh, it was so hard to wait. 'In the meantime,' he'd added, 'I think we need to spend time together.'

She'd been surprised into a laugh. 'Working together the way we do, we probably spend more time together than most married couples!' she'd commented.

'But we don't have the time to learn much about each other on a personal level,' he'd pointed out quietly.

Learning about other people on a personal level was just what she'd spent most of her life avoiding, but one glance at the expression on his face had told her that he wouldn't change his mind.

In the end her decision had been easy to make. If that was what it would take for him to agree, that was what she would do. Secretly, she'd had to admit that the idea had been strangely intriguing.

'Hello?' Sam's voice startled her back to the present and prompted her into hurried speech.

'Sam? It's Kirstin. Sahru's agreed to let me examine her. If she agrees to see you…'

'Well done for getting her that far,' he praised, and she was glad he couldn't see her juvenile response. Blushing at twenty-seven, for heaven's sake! She was a registrar, not an empty-headed ninny! 'Give me a buzz and I'll be there in a minute,' he promised, his calm voice both the cause of and the antidote to her agitation.

'I'm ready.'

The nervous voice from the examining room forced Kirstin to end the call when, for the first time, she'd found herself wanting to prolong it.

The examination didn't take very long and, while she hadn't seen many cases so far, this one was quite severe. Now all Kirstin had to do was persuade the young woman to swallow her mistaken sense of shame and allow Sam to assess the degree of success that could be achieved with an operation.

With an ease born of practice, Kirstin discarded her gloves and pulled the blanket up to her patient's waist then perched herself on the edge of the examining table.

'Sahru, I would like Mr Dysart to examine you,' she suggested carefully.

'W-what? But, why? He—he is a man,' she stammered, her hands clenched tightly on the pale blue blanket as if for protection as she struggled to sit up. The sheen of perspiration picked up by the bright angled light was evidence of how much tension she was already under. 'I have come to you because you are a woman.'

'But *he* would be doing the operation,' Kirstin pointed out, sticking to quiet logic. 'You knew this, didn't you? Hal has told you.' She was almost resorting to holding her breath while she waited, so afraid that she was going to lose Sahru's trust.

'Yes. I know, but this would mean that I must wait again, and I get so nervous as the time for the appointment gets close,' she protested weakly. Kirstin saw her gaze going to the uniform lying neatly folded over the back of the chair as though she longed to be able to escape. 'If *you* cannot do it for me yourself, perhaps it would be best if I just forget it. I have been many years this way, and I am accustomed—'

'Sahru, stop. Listen.' Kirstin took hold of both Sahru's hands to still their agitated fluttering and held tight, waiting till the dark eyes finally met hers. 'You don't have to wait for another appointment because Mr Dysart's ready to come and see you now.'

'*Now?*' she repeated, clearly amazed. 'Sam Dysart is waiting to see me now? But…how? He is so busy that it must take weeks for an appointment.'

'Not for you, Sahru. Not for something as important as this,' Kirstin said in a husky voice, surprised to find herself fighting tears. 'He decided that it was important that you find out *today* what he can do for you, and when he can do it. So…will you see him?'

Now it was Sahru's eyes that were brimming with tears. She was obviously overwhelmed by the whole situation.

'It is Hal who has done this, isn't it?' she choked, unable to meet Kirstin's sympathetic gaze. 'Because his mother had this done to her and was ill so many times, she was determined her daughter would not. For this, his father moved their whole family away from Egypt.'

She looked up with a mixture of fear, shyness and hope on her face. 'He has said that he loves me,' she confided nervously, clearly finding the idea hard to believe. 'And he said it doesn't matter to him if I can never have a child, just so long as he can have me and I am happy.'

'So what do you want to do?' Kirstin prompted. 'Shall I tell Sam to come?' She crossed superstitious fingers and waited.

'Yes. Tell him to come,' she said finally as she lay back on the couch. 'But you must stay here with me, too.'

'I'll even hold your hand, if you want me to,' Kirstin promised with a chuckle of relief, and went to make the call.

'Hello, Mrs Frazer. You're looking *much* better than the last time we saw you.' Kirstin joked as the bed was locked into position in the curtained bay and the nurse transferred the patient's personal belongings to the bedside locker.

After the time spent with Sahru, it had been a rush to get to the ward for hand-over. Apart from his agreement that he would be able to help the suffering woman, there hadn't been time to discuss Sam's findings in detail. There hadn't been time for any conversation of a personal nature either, but the expression in his eyes before they'd parted had told her that somehow he would *make* time.

Her eyes flicked briefly over the chart that had been transferred with Mrs Frazer from ICU, and noted the way the woman's blood pressure had gradually returned to normal after the hasty delivery. The output figures were good, too, suggesting that her kidney function hadn't been permanently impaired. Certainly, the terrible swelling that had affected her whole body was almost completely gone now.

'You certainly made a quick transfer from ICU,' Kirstin commented, making it sound like a compliment. Mrs Frazer would probably never know exactly how lucky she'd been to survive fulminating preeclampsia, and with a healthy child, too.

More than a little of her good luck had been due to Sam's quick thinking and excellent operating technique, she knew, but thoughts about him would have to be banned if she wanted to be able to do her job properly. She was spending far too much time with him on her mind and it was making her uneasy.

'We'll soon have you settled in with us,' she finished brightly as she stowed the notes. 'Is there anything we can do to make you comfortable?'

'They said she's doing well, but…how long will it be before Tamsin…my baby…can join me?' she asked hopefully, wincing as her stitches pulled when she tried to shift her position.

'I'll have a word with Dr Forrester as soon as possible,' Kirstin promised. 'In the meantime, I'll find out how soon we can take you up for a visit.'

'Please! If you can,' the uncomfortable woman said with a pleading expression, her eyes brightened by unshed tears. 'I've only seen her through the window so far—the porter took me for a quick detour on the way here.'

'That's the trouble when you end up with an emergency Caesarean,' Kirstin commiserated. 'You're asleep when they're born so you can't get your hands on them before they're whisked away. Then you're stuck in bed, recovering from your own problems, and neither of you are in a fit state to go visiting each other. Still, hopefully, everything will be back to normal soon. Were you hoping to feed Tamsin yourself?'

The switch in conversation to more practical matters averted the threatened tears and Kirstin was quickly involved in explanations and advice.

It was the same at every bed, each patient wanting to talk, preferably about their new babies. Kirstin had never realised before how easy it could be to find complimentary things to say about each tiny being so it was another hour before she'd completed her round of the postnatal side of the department.

She was relieved to find that, apart from a threatened case of mastitis in a heavily engorged breast, there seemed to be no particular problems brewing.

She made her way to the separate bay at the other end of the unit where they tried to keep the mothers with problem pregnancies as separate as possible from those already enjoying their precious new arrivals.

It didn't happen often, thank goodness, but every so often they would lose a baby, and the last thing the poor mother needed then was to be able to hear the unmistakable sound of healthy infants crying.

The nursing staff had given this little group the all-clear this morning at hand-over, but that didn't mean that one of their 'ladies-in-waiting' wouldn't go into labour at any minute.

Two of them had been in hospital on extended bed rest as a result of threatened miscarriages. They had both reached the stage where their babies were strong enough to survive delivery and were now allowed to move about as much as they liked. It was frustrating and completely typical that neither of them had immediately gone into labour, and both women were heartily fed up with the long wait.

While they'd had each other for company and had obviously become good friends, Kirstin could only imagine what it must have been like for them to be in a hospital bed day after day and week after week. It would probably have driven her round the bend, she admitted silently. She honestly didn't know how the two of them had kept their spirits up so long.

'Still nothing happening?' she asked the two of them sympathetically as she sat on the end of one bed.

'Not a twinge,' Fiona Castle groaned, and glared at the mound which looked as if it would soon completely fill her lap. 'I'm thinking of getting my husband to borrow a motorbike to take me on a cross-country ride. This baby is obviously far too comfortable where it is.'

After her history of miscarriages, Fiona knew that the woman was absolutely over the moon to have come so far with this baby. She'd been seriously worried that she would never be able to carry a baby to term.

'Well, when you've finished with the bike, I want to borrow it. Or how about organising a quick session on a trampoline in the physiotherapy department?' Chelsea Logan chimed in as she looked up from her knitting. 'Do you think that would get something moving?'

'I think you'll have to leave the trampolining until after the delivery, if you don't mind,' said a familiar

voice over Kirstin's shoulder, and she froze while her
heart performed gymnastics.

It was Sam.

She'd been doing so well up until that moment.
She'd hardly thought about the man at all for several
hours, had hardly allowed him into her mind.

Now all she could think about was the intent expression in his eyes when he'd said they needed to
spend time together. She could feel herself start to
blush and hoped the two mums-to-be didn't notice.
She'd never hear the end of it.

'You can't possibly have grown tired of our cui-
sine,' Sam teased them, apparently oblivious of
Kirstin's discomfort. 'And would you be able to guarantee the same sort of room service if you were
home?'

'Maybe not, but at least I'd be able to curl up in
bed with my husband at home,' Fiona said pointedly.
'I don't think your Dr Whittaker would approve if I
did that here.'

The image of curling up in bed with a man brought
with it the shock of her imagination insisting on putting her own and Sam's faces on the two entwined
bodies.

Where on earth had *that* come from?

Even if he *did* decide to help her, that wasn't the
way she intended her pregnancy to be achieved. There
was no way she could allow herself to be put in such
a vulnerable position. Then, why was it that there
wasn't the same attraction when she visualised a plastic beaker and a syringe.

'You wouldn't want to make the rest of the patients
jealous, would you?' Sam retorted, seemingly oblivious to Kirstin's thoughts. 'Anyway, I thought you

were complaining that there was hardly enough room
in the bed for you and the baby. Your husband would
probably end up spending the night on the floor.'

Kirstin was still smiling as she left the little unit.
How was it that Sam always seemed to find the right
thing to say to make their patients feel better? When
they were moaning and getting depressed all she
seemed to be able to do was sympathise with them.
He was able to cheer them up by making them laugh.

Except that he wasn't laughing when he turned to
face her in the wide corridor that ran right down one
side of the department.

'We're due in Theatre in half an hour,' Sam began
with a quick glance at his watch. 'Can you spare a
few minutes to come to my office? In about five
minutes?'

He raised a questioning eyebrow, but her agreement was almost a foregone conclusion.

It would be a miracle if she didn't make a complete
mess of the last couple of items of paperwork, she
thought as she double-checked his latest instructions.
Normally, she had no difficulty keeping her mind on
what she was doing. Nothing was more important to
her than her job.

However, today didn't feel like a normal day and
she was wondering if her life would ever feel normal
again.

If only today was the day when she would find out
if Sam was going to help her to have a baby. Perhaps
it was. Perhaps that was why he'd asked her to his
office.

Hope and apprehension were warring inside Kirstin
as she hurried towards his office. If only he would

say yes, by this time next year she could be holding her own private little miracle.

'Come in,' she heard when she rapped on the pale wood door. She pushed it open, her heart hammering with a mixture of anticipation and dread.

Sam was concentrating on some papers on his desk so she sank into the unattractive chair on the opposite side of his desk and forced herself to wait patiently.

Finally, he looked up and when she met his eyes there was a new expression in them that she didn't recognise.

'Kirstin, I've been thinking,' he began with an air of determination. 'So far, we've only talked about possibilities, of you having a child and of me...assisting you.'

'And?' The word was barely audible as dread began to build inside her. He wasn't going to turn her down now, was he? He'd said he needed time.

'And...' He drew in a sharp breath. 'We've both agreed that there are a host of problems inherent in the situation, not least the fact that I'm your superior in the department.'

'But—' She tried to interrupt but he was determined to have his say.

'The whole situation could become impossible, seeing each other every day with both of us knowing... And then, when it was born...' He shook his head, a frown pulling his dark brows together.

'But I wouldn't expect you to have any responsibility for the child, any more than the other donors on the DI programme,' she hurried to reassure him, surprised to feel a pang of disappointment. She hadn't dreamed that the fact he might see the child he'd fathered would put him off the idea. 'You know I'm perfectly able to support the two of us without assistance. We…we could both sign a legal document or something.'

'You think *that's* what I'm worried about?' he demanded sharply. 'Kirstin, I wasn't worried that you would demand financial help. That's the *least* of my worries.'

He stood up suddenly and began to pace backwards and forwards from the door to the window, his long legs making nonsense of the tiny room.

She'd been startled to hear the pain in his voice and suddenly wondered how many other misconceptions they were holding about each other. If it wasn't the financial aspect that was worrying him, what *was* it?

'I'm still not certain that I'm the right person to do something like this,' he said abruptly. 'You said some very flattering things last night, but why on earth would you want to choose someone like me—with a known impairment that could be inflicted on a child?'

As Kirstin gazed up at Sam she became aware that she'd never realised just how vulnerable a man could be. He could be outwardly successful and confident, but inside…

'Because you're the best man I know,' she countered softly, meaning every word, especially while he was trying so hard to be honourable.

'But you *don't* know me,' he said starkly, coming to a halt just inches from her so that he loomed over her in the office.

For a moment his head was framed against the giant noticeboard on the opposite wall—the one filled with photos of all the healthy babies his department had helped to bring into the world since he'd come to work at St Augustine's.

'You're wrong, Sam,' she said firmly, in spite of the quiver in her voice, and forced herself to straighten up and face him on trembling legs. 'I don't know a single one of the anonymous donors whose contributions are stored in those vats of liquid nitrogen. But *you* I work with every day. *You* I admire...'

She was going to say more, much more, but suddenly there were no more words because she'd been struck dumb by the realisation that she was falling in love with Sam. After all these years of believing that she would never—*could* never fall in love...

The enormity of her discovery was unexpected, frightening, when she'd never intended to allow any man to hold sway in her life.

Kirstin felt so defenceless that for several seconds she actually found herself wishing that she'd never come to Sam for help. If only she'd made an appointment through the usual channels there would have been no emotion-charged meeting when she'd realised that she wanted *him* to be her baby's father.

But what difference would it have made in the end? She would be working with the man at least until the end of her registrarship and that was plenty of time for her to have fallen in love with him, even without the complication of a pregnancy.

Even if he turned her down, she still had the anonymous donors to fall back on, but somehow that prospect had lost its appeal.

'There are other things we need to discuss...things that need to be decided before I could make a decision,' he said quietly, and she subsided onto the chair again.

'For example?' she prompted uneasily.

'Well, you've just pointed out the fact that you're perfectly able to afford to support a child yourself, but does that mean that you would refuse me the right to contribute?'

Something deep inside her twisted with a familiar feeling of fear. She valued her independence and had intended to bring her baby up by herself. She knew that her child would never lack love and was determined that he or she would never know the pain of abandonment.

But there was something in Sam's gaze that spoke of determination, that told her this might be the time for her to see if there was a way to compromise. Sticking to her guns at this point might lose her the child she longed for and she'd come too far now to risk it.

'So what are you suggesting?' Kirstin asked faintly, absolutely certain that she wasn't going to like what he said.

'If I were to father your child, I would want to be a part of his life,' he said firmly, and she was filled with a sudden sinking sensation.

Two hours later, Kirstin was still stewing about their conversation. She'd been prepared to consider a compromise, but Sam's gaze had been so unwavering that she knew it would be hard to change his mind. Anyway, there hadn't been time for that, with patients waiting for their operations.

Sam was less than two feet away but, as ever in Theatre, he was concentrating on the job at hand, taking no more personal interest in her than he did in the scrub nurse standing at his elbow.

The first case on the list had been a routine dila-tation and curettage to remove tissue left in the uterus after a spontaneous abortion. Apparently, it had gone without a hitch, but Kirstin's brain had been so scram-bled by the events of the last half-hour that she'd barely done more than work by rote.

She was ashamed to admit to her lack of attention, knowing it was hardly the professional way to behave when human lives were under her care.

No matter how tangled her personal life, no matter how keen her awareness of the man standing on the other side of the table, her patients deserved her total attention, and from now on they would get it.

This operation, the second on the list, would defi-nitely require all her attention as Sam would be step-ping back into the role of assistant, leaving her in charge. Her patient was a woman in her fourteenth week of pregnancy, and if all went well her procedure should have a rather happier outcome.

After three spontaneous abortions at around the eighteenth to twentieth week of pregnancy, she'd been referred to St Augustine's for investigation of the possibility that she had an incompetent cervix.

The patient's notes had detailed the fact that each of the babies had been the appropriate size for the length of gestation and all had been born alive and normal, although too immature to survive.

The patient was now pregnant again and had come in for the insertion of a Shirodkar's suture to hold the neck of her womb closed. The non-absorbable tape would remain in position until about the thirty-eighth week when it would be removed in preparation for labour.

'How is it looking?' Sam asked, his voice slightly muffled through his surgical mask.

Kirstin glanced up to meet his eyes and realised that he wasn't in the least impassive. She'd never really noticed before exactly how much expression could be conveyed by a pair of eyes over a mask.

Or was it just Sam's eyes?

She could even tell that he was smiling, just by the crinkles at the corners, and she'd never noticed that his eyelashes were quite so long, or so dark...

'Uh, everything's fine,' she said hastily, dragging her attention back where it belonged. 'There was no protrusion of membranes through the cervix, and the tape is lying nice and evenly around it to hold it closed.' She bent for one last look, then stepped back from the table with her hands held up so they wouldn't be contaminated while Sam stepped forward to check her handiwork.

'Neat job,' he said quietly, and she glowed at his praise as she withdrew the speculum and glanced over towards the anaesthetist.

'Ready to bring her up, Hal?'

A general anaesthetic had been required to put the suture in, but was rarely required for its removal.

If all went well, in a little over twenty-four weeks, the tiny being now held safely deep inside would be emerging as a healthy, full-term baby.

Kirstin was just stripping her gloves off and aiming them for the bin when Sam's voice stopped her in mid-throw.

'I'll be waiting for you at the end of your shift,' he stated quietly, considerately making sure they weren't overheard. 'Shall I book a table somewhere, or will you come home with me?'

With so much yet to be resolved, he was obviously certain that she wouldn't object. What he didn't know was the way her heart gave a sudden skip at the prospect of spending time with him, and how much that worried her.

CHAPTER SEVEN

'WELL, done, Mrs Singarajah,' Kirstin praised as she ripped the Velcro apart and put the sphygmomanometer cuff away. 'Your blood pressure is much better this week.'

'My sister has been staying with me,' her heavily pregnant patient explained while she rolled her sleeve down. 'She has been looking after the shop each afternoon while I sit down with my feet up. And I have stopped drinking coffee so much, and I use the substitute instead of salt in my food.'

'Well, it all seems to be working. Keep up the good work!' Kirstin gave her a smile then pushed her way through the curtained cubicle at one end of the consulting room to add her findings to the open file.

This would be Mrs Singarajah's first baby, so her risk of developing pre-eclampsia was higher than with a subsequent pregnancy. The raised blood pressure they'd picked up on her last visit might only have been a symptom of her previous over-indulgence in coffee and salt, but the memory of Mrs Frazer's near-tragedy was still very clear, so Kirstin wasn't taking any chances.

'You are taking your vitamins regularly, aren't you?' she questioned when the young woman appeared from behind the curtain with her clothing rearranged.

'Every day,' the patient said with a determined nod.

'And I will need some more in a few days or I will run out of them before I see you again.'

Kirstin printed up a repeat prescription then made her farewells, glad that she only had two patients left to see in the clinic today.

The fact that those two were Cassie and Naomi meant that she was really looking forward to their visit. The three of them worked so closely within the hospital that they should have almost been tripping over each other, with herself in Obs and Gyn, Cassie in SCBU and Naomi in Paediatrics.

The sad fact was that since her two friends had married they'd seen very little of each other. They hadn't had time to get together for a 'girls' session' since the day Naomi and Cassie had celebrated the discovery that they were due to produce babies within a month of each other.

Mind you, Kirstin thought, that event had been the trigger that had prompted her quest for a child of her own, and ever since then Sam had been monopolising almost every free minute. If she'd had any time to spend with the two of them, they would have been bound to pick up on her preoccupation.

Once upon a time, their visit at the end of a shift would have been a signal that she could afford to let her guard down a little.

Not today.

Today, she would rather not have seen them at all, with the secret she was hiding.

She'd thought long and hard about what she wanted, and over the last few weeks had spoken at length with Sam about all the reasons she was determined to preserve her independence.

There was one topic she couldn't discuss with anyone—the worrying way her feelings for the man just kept growing the more time she spent with him.

After all the time they'd known each other, it felt strange *not* to talk about her worries to Cassie and Naomi, or to Dot, but how could she open her heart to them when she didn't understand her feelings herself?

She knew that Dot wouldn't be happy about what she was hoping to do, and she was certain that her two friends would do their best to talk her out if it. Since their own marriages, they were more convinced than ever that she would eventually change her mind about her decision to remain single.

How could she tell them that she was still as determined as ever that she would never let herself become dependent on a man for her security, and yet wanted desperately to have his child?

The trouble was, today was the very worst day for her to see them because every nerve felt as if it were right on the surface of her skin. To them, it would be a day like any other, with only their visit to the antenatal clinic to ring the changes.

To her, ever since she'd taken her temperature a little over an hour ago and had noted that it had dipped slightly, today had become a day like *no* other.

As soon as Cassie and Naomi had gone she was off duty and she was due to spend the next couple of days with Sam.

She hadn't known that she would enter the most fertile time in her cycle today and that by the time she reached his house her temperature would be slightly elevated, the tell-tale sign that an egg had been released from her ovary and was ready for fertilisation. Neither did she know whether Sam was ready to make his decision yet.

All she could do now was keep her fingers crossed that he would see the timing as a sign that they should go ahead.

Her stomach was full of butterflies whenever she allowed herself to think about what they might be doing this evening, and the closer it got, the less likely she was to be able to hold a coherent conversation.

She closed her eyes and drew in a calming breath. If she didn't get her act together, Cassie and Naomi would definitely know something was wrong, and would badger her until she cracked. Once the two of them got their teeth into something, Torquemada could have learned a thing or two from them when he'd been conducting the infamous Spanish Inquisition.

There was a tap on the door and she had just a second to compose herself before a head of streaky blonde hair appeared around it.

'Are you ready for me?' Cassie asked with a smile, the hard copy of her file in her hand. 'I know I don't really need to see you at this stage, especially as everything's disgustingly normal, but somehow it doesn't feel right just to be checked over by the midwife without seeing you, too.'

'Does "disgustingly normal" mean you're still being sick, or were you referring to your blood pressure, weight and urine tests?' Kirstin asked as she gestured her friend towards the chair.

'It's beginning to ease off a bit, thank goodness, but now that I'm not being so sick I've started putting on weight,' she complained.

Kirstin frowned as she looked for the figures, then

relaxed when she read them. 'Not enough to worry about at this stage. Your body is probably just putting on what it lost when you were throwing up so much.'

'As long as that's all it is,' Cassie said darkly. 'I certainly don't want to end up the size of a house and then have to lose it all after the baby arrives.'

'You're built like a racehorse, so you've always been all long and lean,' Kirstin grumbled. 'You and Naomi have always been able to eat what you liked without putting on an ounce so I doubt you're going to have a problem. Anyway, if you're continuing to work you won't have time for the weight to settle.'

'I hope you're going to give me that as a written guarantee,' Cassie challenged. 'At the moment Luke is hardly letting me move a finger without leaping up to ask if he can do whatever it is for me. He won't even let me pick Jenny up out of her cot. I had to lock myself in the bathroom the other day just to stop him hovering over me.'

'And you're loving every minute of it,' Kirstin accused her, and used a smile to cover the unexpected twist of envy that the mental image provoked. It certainly wasn't that she resented the fact that Luke was being so concerned and protective of her friend. She was actually delighted that Cassie was so blatantly happy.

What she hadn't expected was that she should actually feel a little sad that she would never know that sort of happiness, never have that sort of care lavished on her.

A second tap on the door and Naomi's head came into view.

'Excuse me for interrupting if you're still busy...or have you got to the chatting stage?' she asked.

Kirstin raised an eyebrow in Cassie's direction, leaving her with the decision.

'Come in! Come in,' she invited. 'The more the merrier. I was just having a moan about the fact that Luke wants me to take to my bed like a Victorian lady of leisure and I'm putting on weight.'

'But otherwise you're well?' Naomi asked as she perched one hip on the edge of Kirstin's desk.

Kirstin watched the two of them silently while they swapped horror stories about their symptoms and noted that in spite of their moans they both had that special glow that pregnancy often brought.

She wondered with a growing sense of excitement just how long it would be before she was in the same position, and her thoughts raced ahead.

Would she be one of the lucky ones who conceived at the first attempt? By this time tomorrow, would there already be a small bundle of rapidly dividing cells making their way towards her uterus ready for implantation?

'It would save taking three cars if you travelled with Cassie or me,' Naomi was saying when Kirstin caught up with their conversation.

'Travelled where?' She had obviously lost the thread. 'When?'

'This evening, to visit Dot,' Cassie said patiently. 'The four of us are going, Naomi and Adam, and Luke and I, and as you're not on duty tomorrow, you could come with us. Dot would be delighted to have us all together, and she always makes plenty of food for another one to arrive unexpectedly.'

Kirstin's mind went blank.

What on earth could she say? If they already knew she was off duty, she couldn't use work as an excuse.

And she could hardly say that the reason she wasn't free to visit Dot this evening was because she was hoping to be spending the next two days trying to get pregnant.

'Uh, I can't,' she began, hoping for inspiration. 'I'll be...doing some detailed work on...on donor insemination procedures,' she finished in a rush, hoping they wouldn't ask for specifics.

'Can't you do that tomorrow?' Naomi demanded. 'We don't get many opportunities for all of us to visit her together.'

And if she missed tonight, the most fertile time in her cycle, she would have to wait another month, she thought as her brain whirled in ever-decreasing circles. Would the extra time give Sam more time to make his decision in her favour or would he be more likely to agree if he was presented with the ideal opportunity at short notice?

'But that's the time that Sam Dysart is going to be free,' she blurted, accidentally opting for something that was almost too close to the truth. 'He's giving up his time specially.'

'He's certainly been making you work hard over the last few weeks,' Cassie commented innocently. 'Whenever we've tried to get hold of you, you've been with him.'

Kirstin held her breath, but neither of them seemed in the least suspicious that the time she and Sam were spending together was anything but work-orientated.

'Oh, well,' Naomi said, and shrugged philosophically. 'Another time, then. We'll give Dot your love.'

By the time the two of them left, Kirstin was so on edge that she was almost bouncing off the walls. At the same time, she was so apprehensive that she found herself tidying the files on her desk and even straightening the curtains around the examination couch rather than taking that fateful first step.

'Kirstin? Are you ready?' Sam's voice from the doorway sounded unusually loud in the empty room and she nearly leapt out of her skin.

'Yes,' she said when she could find her voice, her heart beating so fast she could hardly breathe.

'Anything left to do?' he said quietly, leaning one shoulder against the white-painted doorframe. He seemed so totally relaxed that it made her nerves so much worse.

'Um, I've got my bag in my locker,' she said, totally unable to meet his eyes. By coincidence, this was the first time that he'd suggested she stay the night. 'Shall…shall I get it and meet you in the car park?'

'Good idea,' he said easily. 'And I'll need to stop off for some groceries on the way home. You don't mind, do you?'

Mind? She was positively delighted. Anything to delay the moment when she would tell him about the readings on the thermometer and ask him for a decision.

'More wine?' Sam offered, tilting the bottle towards her glass.

'Trying to get me drunk or just relaxed?' she challenged as she leant forward and held the glass towards him, then realised that it must already be working for her to have the nerve to ask.

The quick detour she'd made past the nursery window on her way to meet Sam had certainly helped to calm some of her jitters. She'd stood for several minutes just gazing at the tiny scraps of humanity and had reminded herself that *this* was what she wanted, and Sam was the only man she wanted to help her achieve it.

The babies were so perfect and so helpless, each one a tiny nine-month miracle who would need years of love and worry and care...but she couldn't wait until she had one of her own.

'It's a case of drunk enough to relax or relaxed enough not to need to get drunk,' Sam suggested, putting the bottle down without bothering to top up his own glass. 'Have you had enough to eat?'

She'd drawn the line at oysters when he'd insisted on shopping for a special meal, but everything else must have come from a list of aphrodisiacs in a manual of seduction.

'More than enough,' she groaned, and leant back against the front of the settee again to rest her head on the squashy cushion. If it hadn't been for the food, she would probably have completely lost track of what she needed to tell him...what she needed to ask him.

As it was, they'd started off sitting at either end of the settee, but when he'd started feeding her choice morsels from his own plate they'd gradually moved closer together until they'd eventually migrated to the thick rug on the floor.

They were using the settee for support behind them as they talked about all sorts of topics, both hospital-related and personal.

Kirstin had just thought that she'd never been so relaxed in a man's company when Sam started tempting her with his choice of decadent dessert—strawberries dipped in chocolate.

Her first reaction was to giggle when he stroked the luscious fruit over her lips without allowing her to bite, but then she caught sight of the expression in his eyes. Her breath caught in her throat when she saw the heat and intensity in their dark depths, and suddenly it wasn't a game any more.

'Sam?' she whispered uncertainly, her heart beating faster as her lips became coated in melting chocolate.

'Bite it,' he murmured huskily as he pressed the fruit against her mouth. Unable to resist, she sank her teeth into the soft flesh and the sweet juice exploded over her tongue.

'Mmm,' she groaned in delight and parted her lips for the rest of the strawberry. 'More.'

He was holding onto the green hull so that when she went to bite the second half of the strawberry her teeth grazed his fingertips.

They both froze and suddenly she lost her taste for food.

'Kirstin?' Sam found his voice first but it sounded almost rusty.

There was heat in his gaze and for all her inexperience she was sure that it was evidence that he desired her.

It would be so easy for her to simply let things happen and hope that she became pregnant, but she couldn't do that to Sam. Over the last few weeks she hadn't only come to know him much better but had also managed to fall in love with him. It would be impossible for her to take advantage of a highly charged situation without warning him of the consequences.

Afraid of what he might say, she couldn't look him in the eye, but she forced herself to speak.

'Sam, I wanted… There's something… I thought you should know that… I've been taking my temperature and…'

His whole body grew tense and she knew he'd understood what she was saying.

He was silent for so long that she had to look at him and found he'd been waiting for just that to happen.

'It's gone up?' he asked quietly, his face expressionless but his eyes suddenly almost feverishly bright.

She nodded, biting her lip as she waited to see what he would say. Had the amount of time they'd spent together allayed his fears or would he insist that they wait for another month…or more?

He turned away to drop the forgotten strawberry hull onto a plate, the action only taking on a special significance when she saw the fine tremor in a hand that could wield a scalpel without a qualm.

'Well, then,' he said more softly still, 'I think it's time we went upstairs.'

She hadn't realised that she was holding her breath until it escaped in a rush.

'Are you sure?' she gasped, almost giddy with relief.

'Yes and no,' he said ruefully, and turned to begin collecting the debris from their meal. 'Take your time in the bathroom…have a bath if you like. I'll put this lot away.'

Kirstin was more nervous than she thought she'd be as she scrambled to her feet, and felt as if she went up the stairs like a scared rabbit. The bath helped a little, but there was no way she could enjoy a long soak.

She caught a glimpse of herself in the mirror as she quickly dried herself on the thick white towel Sam had set out for her, and grimaced at the wild curls that had sprung to life in the damp atmosphere.

It wasn't quite as bad as the ginger frizz that had plagued her when she was younger, but it was a far cry from the smooth style she wore to work. Still, there was nothing she could do about it now, or about the fact that her face looked as pale as skimmed milk. It was time to put on the dark green towelling robe that Cassie and Naomi had given her for Christmas and make her way to Sam's bedroom.

She realised that Sam must have been listening to her moving about because almost as soon as she sat down on the side of his bed she heard his footsteps coming up the stairs.

It was almost an anticlimax when she heard the bathroom door close, and she slumped back against the headboard.

There was nothing special about the room, she thought, desperately trying to keep her mind off the sound of running water and her imagination off the thought of Sam's long lean body totally naked...

The room could do with a few decorative touches, something beyond the white walls and ceiling and the French navy curtains and bedding.

The water had stopped and it had all gone quiet. Was he drying himself or was he...?

It would be a shame to cover the rich wooden floor with carpet. Perhaps a sheepskin rug on either side of the bed would be enough, she mused hurriedly, unable to finish her previous thought.

It was so stupid to be like this. She dealt with the specifics of conception and pregnancy every minute of her working life. She knew exactly what process was required to collect sperm from a male donor and it was her own fault if she was now wishing that they were going to make love instead.

After a silence that seemed to have gone on for hours, the sound of the bathroom door opening took her by surprise and she nearly leapt in the air. Uncertain how to greet him, she was on her feet and hovering between the side of the bed and the open door when he appeared.

Kirstin was so wound up that the first thing she noticed was that his dressing-gown was almost the twin of hers. It was several heartbeats later that she noticed that he was standing there empty-handed with a determined expression on his face.

'S-Sam?' she stammered as she glanced from him to the syringe waiting on the plain wooden bedside table. She was sure she'd left the little plastic pot ready in the bathroom.

'I'm sorry, Kirstin,' he said in a gravelly voice, harsh colour high on his cheeks. 'But I want to change my mind.'

'Change your mind?' she said numbly, and stared at him in disbelief. All she could feel for several long moments was a crushing sense of disbelief, but then the anger started to pour in.

'How could you be so…so cruel?' she gasped. 'If you were having second thoughts, why didn't you have the honesty to say so downstairs? Or have you just been leading me on all these weeks? We went through the pantomime of making all those decisions—hospital or home, your place or mine. What did it matter if you weren't going to go through with it?'

She whirled away from him, her tirade collapsing suddenly into gasping sobs, but she refused to let a single tear fall. She hurt too much to be able to bear the additional indignity of letting him see her weeping.

'Kirstin, no!' he exclaimed, clearly horrified. 'It's not like that. Please. Listen.'

She shook her head. What could he say that would mend her shattered dream? To have got this close...

'It's not that I don't *want* to,' he persisted, his voice coming closer until it sounded as if he were just inches away. 'It's that I don't want to do it *that* way.'

Kirstin froze in disbelief. Was he saying what it sounded like? Her heart seemed to be in her throat when she finally made herself turn to face him.

'I haven't actually changed my mind at all,' he confessed softly as he reached out a hand that trembled visibly to touch several strands of the coppery mass tumbling onto her shoulders. 'I've never wanted to do it by any method other than the natural one. I've never liked the idea of my child...our child...being conceived so clinically when there was another way.'

It was almost as if he'd been reading her mind and her sudden blush was so fierce that it felt as if her cheeks had burst into flame.

'You mean you...you're suggesting that we...go to bed together?' she said in a voice made squeaky by disbelief, desperately hoping that she hadn't completely misunderstood.

'If I can remember how it's done,' he said, pulling a wry face. 'It's been some time since I last...' He shrugged, obviously uncomfortable with the admission.

Kirstin was surprised, to say the least. He was a

good-looking man so, if he hadn't had a relationship with anyone for some time, it must be through his choice. Had he, perhaps, made the same decision that she had—to concentrate his energies on his career?

'They say it's like riding a bike—that you never really forget how,' she offered nervously, wondering how she was going to tell him that her own knowledge was purely theoretical.

He smiled and she was pleased to see that it reached all the way to his eyes.

'So,' he whispered as he cupped her cheek in his hand and ran the tip of his thumb gently along her lower lip. 'Shall we go for a ride together and see if we can make a baby?'

Heat was spiralling through Kirstin with every soft touch, turning her insides molten and removing the strength from her knees. Her brain was beginning to shut down all its logical processes but honesty forced her to give him one last chance to change his mind.

'Are you sure you want to do this?' she asked shakily, for a moment not certain what answer she wanted him to give. 'Are you really certain?'

'I'm positive,' he said firmly as his other hand came up to cradle her other cheek and his head began to lower towards hers. 'In fact, *all* of me is positive.'

A *virgin*, Sam thought in amazement as he lay in the darkness with his arms around a sleeping Kirstin. She'd been a virgin until he'd…

He drew in a deep breath and held it, fighting for control. It was either that or let out a Tarzan-like yell. He'd never realised that his male responses could be quite so primitive, but right now he was filled with a mixture of pride, possessiveness and an enormous helping of satisfied ego.

She'd been so sweet and so nervous that he'd been afraid that she was going to change her mind at the last minute. He'd already been beyond that—a long way beyond that, if she'd only realised. Tonight had been the culmination of a fantasy he'd been trying to subdue ever since he'd met the woman, and the fact that it was the first time he'd ever made love without using a condom had made the experience out of this world. And they had a full twenty-four hours before they had to return to work…

He groaned silently, not wanting to wake her again just yet. Well, that wasn't strictly true. He wanted to—he definitely wanted to. In spite of the fact that he was supposedly long past his peak at thirty-five, he had already lost count of the number of times he'd been able to satisfy her in the last few hours. The smug grin he could feel plastered over his face was proof that his fantasy had paled to nothing against the reality of making love to Kirstin Whittaker.

He'd never known that it could be like this, never dreamed that the simple biological fact of joining their bodies together could actually feel as if their souls had been joined, too.

He'd known she was special as soon as he'd met her, and that was something completely separate from her physical beauty. She was dedicated, hardworking, intelligent and genuinely cared about each of their patients.

What he hadn't known until he'd started to get to know her had been that she was also sensitive and strangely lacking in self-confidence as far as her personal life went. For heaven's sake, she actually had no idea of her own striking beauty, with that wealth of dark copper hair against her pale skin and those infinitely changeable greeny-hazel eyes.

And as for her body…

He looked down at the pale slender limbs entwined with his own longer, more heavily muscled ones, and felt the predictable reaction start.

What was it about this woman that he had absolutely no control over himself with her? Perhaps when she became swollen with his child he would finally be able to look at her without reacting like this.

His imagination presented him with a picture of her slenderness grown ripe with the child she carried, her pert breasts swelling as they prepared to nurture it and the pale skin of her belly moving under his hands as he felt the infant moving around inside her. He wasn't going to want her to leave his side in case he missed one precious moment with her.

He heaved a shaky sigh. Even thinking about her heavily pregnant body didn't switch the attraction off, the mental images only increasing his physical discomfort.

'Sam?' she whispered against his throat and his arms tightened reflexively around her as every nerve in his body went on alert.

'Yes?' he whispered against her hair, and drew in the sweet scent that had little to do with soap or shampoo and much more to do with Kirstin herself. 'I'm sorry if I woke you.'

'I'm not,' she countered with a husky chuckle when he felt her brush against the evidence of his arousal. 'I know you advise patients that frequency is one of the best ways to increase your chances of pregnancy, but I never dreamed how often—'

He smothered her teasing with a kiss and a groan when her hand went exploring further. There was no hesitancy now in the way she let him know what she wanted. At first he'd thought that her eagerness had been directed solely towards achieving the pregnancy she wanted. Then, to his amazement, he'd realised that she also wanted him.

Sam was on the verge of sleep when the alarm clock gave one of its periodic clicks and reminded him that they had just six more hours before it would be time to get up for work.

He tightened his arms around Kirstin at the thought that there was so little time left before this magical interlude would end. It was a shock to realise that he wasn't ready for it to end so soon—wasn't ready for it to end at all, if he was honest.

He almost found himself hoping that, in spite of their best efforts, they hadn't achieved their aim. If Kirstin wasn't pregnant, he would be able to look forward to a repeat performance in a month's time, and then the month after that...

Not that he could ever be satisfied with two days in a month. He didn't think he'd have enough of this fascinating woman if he were to make love with her on a daily basis for the next hundred years.

His breath caught in his throat and his eyes flew wide when his silent musings registered properly in his brain.

Make love...for the next hundred years.

Where on earth had that thought come from?

This was supposed to have been a one-off special favour done for a colleague he greatly admired, he thought in sudden panic. It had certainly been the safer option if she was so determined to get pregnant that she'd even contemplated a one-night stand.

He'd known from the outset how highly she prized her independence, but that hadn't stopped him from hoping that he could change her mind. What he hadn't realised was how quickly the situation had got out of hand.

Where did he go from here? Was there a chance that the last twenty-four hours had shown Kirstin that they could have something good together, something permanent, or was he the only one who had ended up with his heart and soul involved?

CHAPTER EIGHT

'KIRSTIN, would you continue for me, please?' Sam said, his deep voice reaching her over the soft sound of a Mozart symphony.

'Of course.' Her words were unnecessary as he immediately set off across the theatre to speak to the colleague waiting anxiously on the other end of the phone.

She hoped she'd managed to hide her delight at his casual vote of confidence in her skill. He wasn't the sort of consultant who took his supervisory duties lightly and would doubtless be keeping an eagle eye on her even from that distance, but even so she was revelling in the warmth it generated around her heart.

She glanced up at him and briefly met the warm smile in his gaze before he angled his head towards the telephone held out for him by one of the theatre nurses. His hands were carefully held away from any danger of contamination and there was a look of utter concentration in his dark eyes as he stared sightlessly across the room.

She returned her own gaze swiftly to the operating field and forced herself to focus on what she was doing, but not before she allowed herself a second to revel in the new intimacy that had developed between them over the last ten days.

How it hadn't become an item of gossip for the whole hospital she didn't know. Sam had even taken to giving her a lift to and from work so that he could spend time with her.

Sternly reining in her thoughts, she set her focus on the work in hand. Her patient had a large fibro-myoma and needed every bit of her skill for its suc-cessful removal.

The fact that she hadn't been able to keep her eyes off Sam ever since they'd spent those mind-boggling two days together wasn't something she was proud of.

That episode had been ten days ago and, unless the test she would be doing in the morning was negative, it was never going to be repeated. She should con-centrate on being thankful that he'd agreed to help her, and stop gazing after him like a lovesick calf.

Kirstin didn't think he'd caught her doing it—at least, she hoped not. It would be so embarrassing, especially when he seemed to be carefully avoiding the topic of their liaison or its results. That didn't mean they didn't find plenty of other things to talk about. He'd even managed to get Mac to trust him at long last...

Irritated that her thoughts had wandered again—this was neither the time nor the place to wonder if Sam wanted to know the result of her pregnancy test—she concentrated on a mental review of Mrs Lattimer's case history leading up to her presence on the table.

A high-flying career-woman who hadn't started try-ing for a family until her early thirties, she'd initially thought she'd fallen pregnant when the waistbands of her clothes had quickly become too tight. The bouts of uterine pain and intermittent bleeding had brought her to Sam and a battery of tests.

An ultrasound scan had brought the bad news that she hadn't been pregnant after all, and a follow-up X-ray had confirmed the diagnosis of a tumour, but it hadn't been until the lab tests had been done on tissue samples that an endometrial carcinoma had been ruled out.

The mass was large enough that if Mrs Lattimer hadn't still been so keen to have a family she would have been advised to have a hysterectomy. As it was, Sam had offered to try to shell the fibroid out from the myometrium by myomectomy. If the operation was successful, when she had fully recovered she could try again to conceive the longed-for baby.

Kirstin sighed with relief as she finally lifted the dense mass out and deposited it into the dish held ready by an anonymous hand, then bent closer to check once more that she hadn't missed anything. She was concentrating so hard that she hadn't realised Sam had returned to the table until he spoke.

'Nice, neat job,' he commented quietly as the ends of the last internal stitch were clipped, his voice emerging into the pause between movements in the Mozart symphony so that the whole team heard the praise.

Kirstin hoped her mask covered enough of her face so that everyone couldn't see how much his words had affected her. It wasn't the first time she'd had cause to curse her pale skin and its tendency to colour so easily.

Sam had commented on it when he'd apologised for marking her with his newly emerging beard, and had insisted on having another shave straight away. He'd then insisted on rubbing his face all over her so she could tell him if he'd done a good enough job…

'Ready to reverse the anaesthetic?' she asked, grateful that her thoughts hadn't wandered again until she'd all but completed the operation. She could only hope and pray that once she had the answer to the test in the morning, her brain would return to its normal orderly function. If she was going to be this easily distracted by the man, she might have to reconsider applying for a permanent position with him.

She stifled a groan behind her mask. Even her most innocent work-related thoughts seemed to have taken on a life of their own. Just the phrase 'applying for a permanent position with him' had brought lascivious images into her head.

It was time this stopped, she warned herself sternly as she stripped her gloves off and flung them into the bin. If not, she could become a danger to her patients. Then she'd have no way to earn a living for herself and the child she might already be carrying.

'Kirstin, when you've checked on Mrs Lattimer in Recovery, would you come to my office to give me an update?' Sam asked. 'That phone call was to tell me one of our IVF patients is on her way in. It looks as if she might be miscarrying.'

His request was unusual when the information could easily have been given on the ward or by phone, but no one except Kirstin seemed to have noticed.

She glanced at him quickly but this time there was absolutely nothing in his expression to make her think that he had anything personal on his mind.

Even so, she had a strange feeling as if she was waiting for something to happen, something completely separate from the results of the test in the morning.

It was nearly an hour before she finally knocked on Sam's door and she half wondered if he might have given up waiting for her. Still, if she couldn't page him, she could always leave him a note.

She refused to acknowledge the sudden lift to her heart when she heard his voice bidding her to enter.

'I'm sorry to be so late,' she began almost before the door clicked shut behind her, 'but I've only just left Mrs Lattimer. It took rather a long time before she came out of the anaesthetic so I stayed to tell her that the operation went well.'

'It did indeed,' he said quietly as he came round to the front of his desk and perched one hip on the corner. 'Take the weight off your feet—I don't expect you've sat down for hours. And you responded very well to being dumped in at the deep end at short notice. It was a very neat piece of work. If there are no unexpected problems with fertility levels, I reckon Mrs Lattimer still stands a good chance of being able to fall pregnant.'

Instantly, Kirstin grew tense. It was inevitable, really, with the topic so much on her mind, and when he met her gaze she realised that it was on his as well, in spite of the fact he hadn't mentioned it once in the last ten days.

'Any news yet?' Sam asked with a telling strain in his voice. 'Have you done a home test or have you decided to have it done here?'

'I—I bought one of those kits,' she said with a slight hitch in her voice, unexpectedly emotional with the realisation that he did care. 'I was going to do it at home tomorrow morning…unless you think it would be more accurate here?'

'It's probably as broad as it's long, except that here

there's always a slight risk that someone might make a connection to your name. Have you told your friends what we…you're trying to do?'

Kirstin tried to subdue a shudder at the thought of her private business becoming grist for the voracious gossip mill at the hospital. If it ran true to form, just the slightest hint would be enough to spread the story, with embellishments added at every stop.

'I haven't told anyone—not even Cassie and Naomi.' Partly because she was certain that the two of them would have tried to dissuade her, but also because the whole idea was so new, the prospect of motherhood so exciting that she wanted to hug it to herself for a while. She didn't even know if there was anything to tell them yet—other than the fact that she'd enlisted Sam's help.

'In spite of patient confidentiality, being a member of staff sometimes seems to make people forget the rules. I think I'd rather do it in the privacy of my own bathroom than risk that,' she decided, then paused to add tentatively, 'Did…do you want to know the result?'

'Of *course* I want to know,' he said emphatically. 'Why on earth would you think I didn't?'

'Well, it's just that you haven't mentioned it since…so I wasn't sure whether you…' she finished uncertainly.

'Kirstin, for the sake of your reputation I've tried to keep our dealings as normal as possible. But at some stage, when you tell people you're pregnant, someone is going to do their arithmetic. I didn't want to give the gossips anything to get their teeth into if they remembered that around this time we were seen to be sharing lots of secretive whispered conversations.'

'Oh,' she breathed, and felt a smile spread over her face as understanding dawned.

'So, how have you been feeling? Any different?' he quizzed, and she laughed.

'Hardly! Even if I *am* pregnant, at ten days it's barely recognisable as an embryo yet. Anyway, I usually have a bit of breast tenderness just before my period's due, so that's no criterion.'

As soon as she mentioned the symptom, she regretted it. Somehow it was completely different when she was talking to him like this about a patient. Then his eyes didn't go to her breasts and make them tingle with remembered pleasure.

She wanted to fold her arms to hide the fact that her body was responding to his gaze, but she was still wearing theatre scrubs and the well-washed cotton would just make her reaction more obvious.

She almost breathed a sigh of relief when the phone rang and she was about to make her escape when she heard him swear softly, and paused.

'Mrs Thrush lost the babies,' he announced bluntly as he dropped the receiver back down with a clatter, and Kirstin's heart fell. No one on the unit liked to admit failure, especially for someone like Mrs Thrush who had been through so much.

'What happened this time?' She curled her fingers around the top of the chair and gripped tightly. For some reason she'd become especially attached to the courageous woman, and not just because they shared the same colour hair.

Her first pregnancy had resulted in a full-term still-birth and her second had been ectopic and had resulted in the loss of one of her Fallopian tubes. Two more early miscarriages had been followed by another ectopic which had disastrously robbed her of her remaining Fallopian tube.

With her two still functioning ovaries no longer viably connected to her uterus, her only option had been IVF, so her eggs had been harvested and fertilised outside her body, then returned to her uterus for implantation.

Neither embryo had implanted on the first attempt and now, twelve weeks after an apparently successful implantation, she had just lost twins.

'Anything significant?'

Sam shook his head. 'She just started spotting and cramping a few hours ago. Her husband rushed her in but it was probably already too late. That phone call was the result of the scan. No foetuses and no heartbeats.'

For the first time Kirstin could begin to appreciate the misery the mothers went through when this happened. All she had to do was imagine how she was going to feel tomorrow morning if the test told her she wasn't carrying Sam's baby. How much worse must it be when the baby had already started to kick?

Suddenly she felt a strong need to be held and wished that she had the right to be able to ask Sam for a hug.

That would be all very well if the two of them had that sort of relationship, but they didn't. They were both loners by choice and she couldn't imagine what he would make of such a demand. And she *didn't* want to make demands, because relying on anyone other than herself was a sure way to get her heart broken.

'I'd better get back to the wards and check every-one over before the end of my shift,' she said weakly, suddenly needing to put some distance between her-self and Sam.

'Who on earth is that?' Kirstin asked aloud early the next morning when the buzzer by the front door of her flat sounded before her alarm had even gone off.

In spite of the fact that it had taken her a long time to get to sleep, she'd woken early with just one thing on her mind.

She'd still been lying huddled under the covers and steeling herself for that fateful trip to the bathroom. It was far too early for the postman to be leaving any parcels, and she certainly wasn't expecting any visi-tors at this time of the morning.

'Who is it?' she demanded a minute or two later, finding the button on the intercom in spite of a wild mane of sleep-tumbled hair.

'Sam,' said the disembodied voice. 'I've brought breakfast.'

'Breakfast?' she repeated with a crazy leap of her heart, completely forgetting to press the button to speak.

'Are you going to let me in?' he demanded. 'I've got croissants.'

She didn't need his coaxing tone to remind her of the last time she'd eaten the flaky pastries with Sam... in his bed the first morning after they'd...

And he'd found some interesting ways of sharing the last one with her.

She pressed the other button on the intercom box and the harsh buzz told her that the downstairs lock had been released. Only then did she suddenly realise that she was standing in her tiny hallway in a threadbare old T-shirt with her hair like a rat's nest.

Before she'd taken more than two paces towards her bedroom to remedy the situation, there was a knock at her door.

'What did you do? Run all the way up the stairs?' she grumbled as she released the catch then scooted out of sight to find her towelling robe.

'I didn't notice you being this grouchy the last time I brought you croissants for breakfast,' he said mildly, and she poked her tongue out at him from behind the closed door. It didn't matter that he couldn't see it, she knew that she'd done it.

She reached for her hairbrush but the first thing she saw was the neat pink and blue box waiting for her to take it into the bathroom.

She closed her eyes and groaned silently, tension making her feel slightly sick. She knew that she couldn't put it off any longer, so she grabbed the box and stuffed it in the pocket of her towelling robe.

'I'm just going to the…bathroom,' she finished as she nearly ploughed into Sam on his way out of her tiny kitchen.

'I didn't know whether you might want this.' He diffidently held out a small box—a different brand, but nevertheless another pregnancy testing kit. 'I thought, whatever the result is, you wouldn't be absolutely convinced that it was right. So if you do two tests at the same time, you can check it straight away.'

'Thank you.' Slow heat crawled up her throat and into her face as she held her hand out, but she was glad he'd thought of it. She hadn't realised that he'd grown to know her so well. But how else could he have known that she would probably disbelieve whatever result the first kit gave her?

The fact that he had turned up at all told her that he was almost as impatient as she was to know the result, or was it that he'd guessed she might need some supportive company? Whatever his reasons, the thing she hadn't expected was that she would be quite so pleased to have him here.

'I've put the croissants to warm. They'll be ready when you've finished,' he said with an encouraging smile before he turned to retrace his steps to the kitchen. 'You've got a choice when you're ready— I've brought apricot jam or strawberries to go with them.'

The thought of strawberries was enticing as she shut herself in the bathroom. She didn't think she'd ever forget the last of the chocolate-covered ones they'd shared in his bed in the middle of the night.

Her hands were trembling visibly while she struggled to open both boxes, then she had to force herself to read the instructions carefully before carrying them out to the letter.

In the dreadful minutes while she was waiting for the results she gave her teeth a brushing that would have made her dentist proud and her hair a brushing that would have had her hairdresser screaming.

Then the wait was over and it was time to make herself look.

Pregnant!

Both kits said that she was pregnant!

For just a split second her heart sank with disappointment that she wouldn't have the excuse to ask Sam to go to bed with her again, but then the enormity of the positive results washed over her.

Protectively, she placed both hands over her belly as though to cradle the minute being already developing inside her.

'A baby,' she whispered as her eyes started to fill with emotional tears. 'I'm really going to have a baby.'

A clatter in her kitchen reminded her that Sam was still out there, making breakfast for her and waiting to know the results.

It had been so kind of him to think of coming, especially bringing a duplicate test and breakfast. Until this moment she hadn't realised just how important it was going to be to share her news with someone instead of having to keep it all to herself.

'Sam, look!' she called as she opened the bathroom door with an indicator in each hand. 'Look at these!'

He must have been waiting for the sound of the door because he was at her side in an instant, bringing with him the pungent smell of freshly brewed coffee.

Immediately, the faint queasiness she'd put down to nerves became imperative and she whirled back to the bathroom, desperately hoping she'd reach the toilet before she was sick.

'Sam, you can't keep doing this. It's ridiculous!' Kristin moaned after she'd rinsed her mouth out with the glass of water he'd handed her and wiped her face with the cool flannel.

'Why not?' he demanded as he helped her to her trembling feet then followed her out of the bathroom. 'Admittedly, it wasn't my first choice, but it's better than the other alternative. Look at it from my point of view—at least this way you stand a chance of arriving for work on time.'

Kirstin groaned as she slumped onto the end of her bed and accepted the triangle of dry toast he offered her.

She hadn't got the energy to argue with him. This ghastly morning sickness had only been going on for a couple of weeks so far and there could be another two months of it to go. The only good part about it was that it seemed to be confined to the first hour or so after she woke up.

Sam's first suggestion, when he'd realised just how badly she was being affected, had been that she should move into his house.

'The sickness won't last so long if you can get something into your system before you move,' he'd pointed out. 'It would be so much easier if I could just bring it to you in bed without having to trail around the streets first.'

In the most secret corner of her mind, Kirstin had to admit that just for a heartbeat or two she'd actually been tempted by the idea. There had been something very enticing about the idea of living in the same house as the man she'd fallen in love with—the father of her baby. They might even be able to spend time together when she was feeling well enough to enjoy it.

Then self-preservation had kicked in and she'd remembered all the reasons why she couldn't allow herself to become dependent on Sam, or any other man.

She might have won the argument about staying in her own little flat but she certainly hadn't won the battle over stopping him arriving each morning. If only he hadn't been right about the need to get something into her system before she started moving, she might have stood a better chance of discouraging him.

The trouble was, there were so many other reasons why it would have been a good idea to move into his house while she was being so sick. For a start, she genuinely liked him. She enjoyed his company as a man and admired him as an obs and gyn consultant. She also liked his house, bare as it was, and not just because of the earth-shattering memories they'd made there. More than once she'd found herself imagining the way it could look if she had a free hand to add a few finishing touches—not that *that* was very likely.

Unfortunately, there had been other considerations to be taken into account when she'd been weighing up her options and the other side of the coin was a very different matter.

One of the most important was the fact that once her pregnancy became common knowledge, people were far more likely to put two and two together if she was living in Sam's house.

Kirstin still wasn't certain what the powers that be at the hospital would think if they heard that their eminent consultant had fathered the baby of his registrar, a woman eight years his junior. It would be unbearable if the gift he'd given her was to result in the destruction of his career.

Then there was the personal angle.

She was coping with having to accept his help because, so far, it had all been confined to her own territory. If she were to move into his house, not only would they be working together but they would also be spending every off-duty moment together.

In spite of all her years of determination, she could see that it would be a recipe for heartbreak.

The one thing she had to remember was that it was her only-just-there baby causing all this upset. Things were going to get very much more complicated a little further down the road after the birth, and she needed plenty of practice at coping with things alone. If she didn't insist on standing on her own two feet right from the start…

Standing on her own two feet? She gave a hollow laugh as she forced herself to collect the clothes she'd set out for herself last night and made her way back to the bathroom for her shower.

Over the last two weeks she'd learned the hard way how important it was to do as much organisation as possible before she went to bed. In the morning she'd rather curl up in a ball and die than start sewing on buttons, cleaning her shoes or finding a pair of un-damaged tights.

Stand on her own two feet? The way she felt at the moment, she wouldn't be standing at all if it hadn't been for Sam arriving each morning to take care of her.

'Hey, Kirstin, what's this I hear about you and Sam?' Naomi demanded with a gleeful grin, almost bouncing with excitement as she cornered her friend in the corridor.

'That depends on what you've heard,' Kirstin countered as she tried to find a way of escaping. She'd seen that expression on her friend's face before, and knew it promised a long and detailed interrogation. Trapped in a corner the way she was…

'I've been told that you don't have to walk back-wards and forwards to the hospital any more—that he's taken to giving you lifts. Cassie saw you getting out of his car yesterday morning. *And* you weren't at your flat to answer your phone when I rang first thing

this morning. Are the two of you *an item*?' she asked
with pointed emphasis. 'Are you thinking about moving in with him, or have you done it? I got your answering machine this morning when I rang.'

'Oh, that was *you* this morning, was it? Why didn't
you leave a message? I was only in the bathroom, but
by the time I got there you'd rung off,' Kirstin said
quickly, trying to forget exactly what she'd been doing in the bathroom at the time. She certainly wasn't
going to have to worry about putting on any tell-tale
weight while this morning sickness continued.

'Oh.' Naomi's face fell. 'I put two and two together
when you didn't answer. I was really hoping you'd
ditched your old prejudices to take a chance on him.
He might be quiet and a certifiable workaholic but
he'd be almost delicious enough to tempt me if I
didn't already have Adam.'

'Naomi, how many years have I been telling you
that I won't be getting married?' Kirstin reminded her
impatiently, and reminding herself at the same time.
The more she saw of Sam and the more she learned
about him, the less fearsome the prospect became, and
therein lay the danger.

'Ah, but getting married isn't the same as moving
in together,' Naomi said gloatingly. 'And Cassie *did*
see you getting out of his car.'

'Did she also notice that the rain was absolutely
bucketing down at the time? Did she also know that
Sam lives a couple of streets away from my flat and
that, as he drives right past my door, he picked me
up out of the kindness of his heart? What would she
want him to do—drive past and leave me to wade
through it for fifteen minutes?'

Kirstin felt uncomfortable with the whole conversation. She wasn't in the habit of lying, but in this case she was only stretching the truth a little. She *wasn't* living with Sam and he *could* drive right past her door if he chose that route to the hospital.

The fact that he was actually coming to her flat each morning to try to help her through the ghastly morning sickness was something she wasn't ready to tell anyone yet.

'Darn it,' Naomi grumbled with a disgruntled pout. 'We were really hoping that you'd finally succumbed.'

'We?' Kirstin repeated. 'Succumbed to what?'

'Cassie, Dot and me, of course,' Naomi said impatiently. 'We hoped you'd finally found someone who could make you change your mind. I'm sure if you were to let him get closer, Sam would be able to persuade you to have a baby or two for him.'

It was a typically outrageous Naomi-type statement but it took Kirstin's breath away.

Let Sam get closer? The way they'd been for those twenty-four hours, they couldn't have got any closer. And it hadn't been Sam who'd persuaded her to carry his baby.

'Don't hold your breath,' she advised Naomi wryly while she tamped down the nasty feeling of regret that was becoming her companion. 'You and Cassie are happy with Adam and Luke and I'm very happy for you, but you've always known my feelings about being dependent on anyone. You know I'd never allow anyone to get that close to me—to allow myself to be that vulnerable.'

Her voice had risen a little as she'd said the words and she was suddenly conscious that they could have been overheard by anyone along this stretch of corridor.

Her overdeveloped sense of privacy had her looking both ways to see if anyone *had* heard, then the door behind her opened and she found herself looking right into the accusing dark eyes of Sam Dysart.

CHAPTER NINE

'KIRSTIN, may I talk with you?' Sahru Ismail asked hesitantly, catching her in the corridor on her way to find some food.

'Of course,' Kirstin said with a smile, glad that *someone* wanted to talk to her.

It had been almost a week since Sam had overheard her conversation with Naomi and, while he hadn't mentioned it, he'd become more distant with her.

The crazy thing was, he was still turning up each morning to make her some toast in an attempt to avert her nausea, and handing her a glass of water and a cool flannel when she stopped being sick.

She really didn't understand the man.

From his expression last week, it had almost looked as if her words had hurt him, and yet there had never been anything...intimate or personal between them other than those forty-eight hours at his house. They had never made any promises so there were none to break, but perhaps she had said or done something that had allowed him to make assumptions. Had she somehow let slip the fact that she'd made the mistake of falling in love with him? Whatever it was, something had obviously gone badly wrong.

She hadn't realised that he'd become a friend until the openness of that friendship had been withdrawn.

'I wanted to speak with you because you were so patient with me when I came for the consultation,'

Sahru said shyly. 'I wanted you to know that I will be having the operation.'

'Oh, Sahru, that's wonderful news,' Kirstin exclaimed, absolutely delighted. 'When? Soon?'

'Tomorrow. In the morning,' she whispered with a flicker of fear, and reached for Kirstin's hand. 'Please, is it possible that you could be with me? I'm still very frightened.'

'You may be frightened, but you're still going through with it. I'm so proud of you, Sahru,' she said, and squeezed the trembling fingers. 'It'll be Sam Dysart doing the operation, so you've got nothing to be frightened about. If the operation is tomorrow, I'll be seeing you on the ward later on today, probably about teatime, to do your pre-op work-up. I'll also be in the theatre tomorrow, assisting, so I'll be with you right through the operation.'

'Thank you so much.' Sahru drew in a shuddering breath and managed a shaky smile. 'I have no other friends here, because all my family are in Sudan.'

'What about Hal?' Kirstin suggested, knowing how the young Egyptian anaesthetist felt about his beautiful colleague. 'I'm sure he would want to be with you.'

'Because of my background it still feels *wrong* for a man who is not a husband to be involved in female matters. Anyway, at the moment I don't really want to see Hal because I feel like strangling him,' Sahru muttered with feeling, her large dark eyes slitted balefully. 'If it was not for him, I would not be going through this.'

Kirstin chuckled. 'Just concentrate on how much happier you're going to feel when it's all over, how much better your life will be. And you'll be able to look forward to a relationship with Hal.'

Kirstin had been watching the changing expressions on the young woman's beautiful face and couldn't help seeing the fear that her last suggestion brought.

'I do not know if I will ever be able to do this,' Sahru said softly, regretfully.

'Oh, Sahru.' Kirstin's heart went out to her. 'Don't think about that yet,' she advised gently, hoping Hal knew what he was taking on. Sahru was so vulnerable that if he were to reject her after the trauma she was about to be subjected to, Kirstin didn't know if the poor woman would survive. 'Just concentrate on getting the operation over, and then see what happens. If he loves you and you love him, I'm sure you'll be able to sort something out. There's much more to a relationship than what does or doesn't happen in the bedroom.'

Their conversation was rudely interrupted by the imperative summons of a pager, and Kirstin groaned.

'That's for me. I'll have to run, Sahru, but I'll see you later. OK?'

'OK,' Sahru echoed as Kirstin took off towards the nearest phone.

'Sometimes I really don't like my job,' Kirstin muttered an hour later as she tried to work the kinks out of her shoulders.

'You're regretting specialising in obs and gyn?' Hal asked in surprise. She saw him throw a glance in Sam's direction, but there was no comment forthcoming in spite of the fact that he was obviously listening. 'But I thought you loved it.'

'I do, but sometimes I wonder if I'd love the child-birth part more if I were a midwife. I only seem to see the problems and the tragedies while they get all the easy births.'

'Ah, but when you have one like Mrs Caistor that you really have to struggle over, don't you feel a greater sense of satisfaction when it all comes right in the end?' Sam's voice was soft but it was full of conviction and she knew that he must be voicing his own feelings. At least he was still speaking to her in a work context.

'Yes, it's a fantastic boost,' she agreed readily, 'but at the time, when it looks as if we're going to lose mother and baby, it just makes me feel sick. It's almost as if I'm trying to run through treacle—I just can't seem to do enough things fast enough to help them. I feel so inadequate, as if I'll never know enough.'

'We all feel like that at times, Kirstin,' Hal said with a chuckle. 'It doesn't matter how long we've been doing the job.'

'He's right,' Sam agreed, but his face was very serious. 'There will always be cases where we try to fight nature, and lose. For one reason or another, it's almost a daily occurrence in the IVF unit: women whose problems are beyond our help; women who can only ever get so far before they lose their babies; women whose babies are born prematurely or mal-formed; women who crack under the physical and emotional stress of going through it time after time only to be disappointed.'

Kirstin watched, almost mesmerised, as his tumble of words revealed some of the passion he hid behind his studious workaholic outer shell.

'As far as Mrs Caistor is concerned, Kirstin, the only way you could have done anything better or faster is if you were Superwoman. That cord prolapse could have meant a brain-damaged baby. You did an excellent job of maintaining his blood supply while you untangled everything so she didn't need an emergency Caesarean.

'The only injuries were a few bruises and some stitches which will make Mrs Caistor sit a bit gingerly for a few days. But, considering that she's ended up with a perfect, healthy baby boy, I'm certain she'll forgive you for the discomfort.'

As Sam strode out of the room, Hal gave her a grin and a thumbs-up sign, but she didn't need it. After that sort of fulsome praise she was almost floating around on a little pink cloud, especially as it had come from Sam.

'I'd better go with you while you check up on her in Post-Op,' Kirstin muttered in a determined attempt at getting her feet back on the ground. It was all very well for Sam to heap commendations on her in Hal's presence, but they still hadn't begun to resurrect the friendship she'd once enjoyed.

It was so frustrating. Each morning he was spending at least an hour with her, but she wasn't in a fit state to hold much of a conversation with him. For the rest of the day he seemed to be annoyingly successful at avoiding her whenever there was a chance they might be alone together.

Enough was enough, she decided as she made her way to the office to do battle with yet another Everest of paperwork. They were going to be virtually joined at the hip all day tomorrow, with a full operating list. The last thing she wanted was to spend all that time watching every word she said. It was time she pinned him down and cleared the air between them, even if it meant going round to his house this evening.

Kirstin had never been so glad to see bad weather before. Just a glance out of the window was enough to tell her that, if anything, the rain was worse than this morning. And if Sam held true to form, that meant he would insist on giving her a lift home.

Bearing in mind the fact that she shared her building with several other people, she would rather their discussion took place in the greater privacy of *his* house, but one way or the other she was going to speak to Sam, even if she had to force him to listen.

She was primed for battle when he did, in fact, insist, so it was almost a letdown when he waited until she'd fastened her seat belt to speak.

'We need to talk, Kirstin,' he announced bluntly, apparently fascinated by the water streaming down the windscreen. 'Will you come home with me or would you prefer that I take you to your flat?'

She was relieved that he'd finally recognised the need to clear the air, too, but had to pause a second to swallow down the lump of dread that had lodged in her throat. 'Your house would be better—less chance of neighbours eavesdropping,' she suggested.

Without another word he started the engine and drew away, every movement ruthlessly efficient and fascinating to watch even in the intermittent light.

'If you wait, I'll get an umbrella,' he suggested as he drew up in his drive.

'It's not worth it for the sake of a few yards,' she pointed out, and let herself out of the car.

'Tea, milk, juice or water?' he offered as he led

the way to the kitchen. 'Keep your coat on for a few minutes while I turn the heating up.'

While he dealt with the controls she went to the cupboard to take a glass out for some juice, taking a grim pleasure that she'd actually come to know his kitchen well enough to know where they were kept. That had happened during the days when he'd invited her to spend time with him.

'Did you want some?' she asked as she poured and suddenly realised that to an outsider it would have looked like a thoroughly ordinary domestic scene. She was surprised at the sharp pang around her heart when she reminded herself sternly that it wasn't the sort of scene she was ever likely to participate in.

She knew from bitter experience that nothing lasted—not relationships, not families, not promises. All of them disintegrated sooner or later and all that was left was pain and disillusionment.

Far safer to steer clear, far safer not to rely on any-one else for support, then you couldn't be let down, couldn't be hurt. Except she'd done her best to remain independent and she was *still* hurting.

She saw Sam's hand hovering over the jar of coffee but then he threw a quick glance in her direction and she was grateful to see that he passed on to the tea. Obviously he'd remembered that even at this time of night she didn't seem to be able to stand the smell of coffee.

'The sitting room should have warmed up by now, or would you rather stay in here?'

Sam's voice was almost expressionless but she could see that he was fighting hard to suppress a vol-cano of emotion. If she were to sit at the table in here, they would be just inches apart. At least in the sitting room she would be a little further away from him if he finally exploded.

'Let's be comfortable,' she suggested blandly and led the way, hoping he couldn't tell how tense she was.

It was stupid, really, to be so nervous of him *now*. This was the same man with whom she'd spent forty-eight of the most exquisite hours of her life. Since then, he'd spent far too many mornings supporting her and yet she still didn't feel she knew him.

They both sat down in silence, one on either end of his settee, and each silently drank several mouthfuls as though waiting for the other to begin.

Finally, Sam spoke.

'I know it's rather late in the day to ask, but I need to know exactly what your intentions are,' he said in quiet, measured tones that didn't match the tension visible in his jaw.

'My intentions?' Kirstin replied, not understanding what he meant. He sounded almost like a Victorian father interviewing his daughter's suitor.

'Yes. Your intentions,' he reiterated sharply. 'How much longer are you going to go on like this? You won't move in with me to let me do anything to help you, so I'm limited to holding your head in the mornings. You haven't told any of your friends about the baby—even Cassie and Naomi,' he pointed out fiercely, 'so you can't call on them to help you either.'

He gestured at her, his dark eyes raking her from head to toe and telling her he didn't like what he was seeing.

'You're losing weight, dammit,' he continued angrily, 'and looking so fragile that a stiff breeze would blow you over. When are you going to admit that even someone as independent as you just can't do it all on your own, that you need help?'

'I don't,' she objected, her pride stung. 'At least, I won't once the sickness stops. It'll only be a few more weeks and I'll probably start blowing up like a balloon. There's plenty of time for me to make up the little bit I've lost.'

He glared at her, obviously not satisfied but equally obviously aware that there was nothing he could do if she wouldn't let him.

'So why haven't you told anyone about the baby yet?' Sam demanded, striking in a different direction. 'I thought you, Cassie and Naomi were so close? Why the big secret about your pregnancy when they're sharing every detail of theirs with you?'

'I… Well, I just…just wanted to savour it for a while first,' she said weakly, having questioned herself on exactly the same topic only the previous night.

There was a certain amount of truth in her answer, but she'd been shocked to realise that there was also an element of shame in her desire for secrecy.

It was all very well for Cassie and Naomi to flaunt their pregnancies. They were both married and everyone was only too willing to congratulate them.

It would be a completely different matter when they found out about *her* baby. Some of society's mores might have changed over the last century, but there would always be a shadow over an illegitimate pregnancy, no matter how polite people were to her face.

The silence between them grew until it almost seemed to take on a form of its own. Kirstin had finished her juice but was still clutching the empty glass like a lifeline.

Sam had abandoned his tea on the corner of the coffee-table, apparently too worked up to drink it.

She could see the turbulence in his dark eyes and in the tension in his shoulders and the white-knuckled fists clenched between his knees.

The explosion came from a totally unexpected direction and nearly broke her heart.

'Have you changed your mind?' he demanded suddenly, harshly, his lean, clever face looking almost gaunt.

'Changed my mind? About what?' It was impossible to drag her gaze away from the sight of so much pain.

'About having the baby…because it's mine. Because of the dyslexia. Have you decided you don't want it after all?'

The words were coming at her in short bursts, like machine-gun fire and with the same deadly effect. For a moment it felt as if her heart had stopped and she could barely draw breath.

'You think…that I haven't told anyone because I'm thinking of *aborting* the baby?' Kirstin gasped in shock, finally understanding the enormity of the fear he'd been living with. She put a protective hand over the as yet non-existent bump. 'How can you think that I would want to do that?'

'What else *can* I think?' he retorted, his frustration getting the better of him as he leapt to his feet and started to pace. 'You haven't wanted anyone else to know anything about it—not your friends, or your colleagues—so they'd never know it had ever existed.

'You've only spoken about my role in the child's future in the vaguest of terms, in spite of the fact that if you continue to work at St Augustine's we'll probably be seeing each other on an almost daily basis for years to come. You even argue with me about wanting to help you out with something as simple as a glass of water and a flannel.'

He came to a halt right in front of her, towering over her as she sat on the seat in front of him like a petrified rabbit.

'It's my child, too, even if you'd rather forget the fact,' he declared forcefully. 'And that means I have the right to know if you've decided to get rid of it.'

Kirstin could empathise with his feelings of vulnerability—she'd been in that position too many times in her life not to recognise it. That didn't mean that she could control her red-headed temper when it responded to the accusation.

'Back off!' she commanded furiously, glaring up at him, and when he did, shot to her own feet.

'How could you *possibly* believe that I would kill this baby?' she demanded, a hand held protectively over it. 'Have you forgotten what I was prepared to do to get it? Have you forgotten what I *did* do to get it? It can hardly have escaped your notice that my mornings for the last few weeks have been anything but a picnic. If I were going to get rid of the baby, why haven't I done it already? Why would I be putting myself through misery?'

Now it was her turn to pace, and for once she was glad that he had so little furniture. She was so angry that she needed plenty of space.

'You want honesty?' she continued harshly. 'All right, I'll give you honesty. You want to know why I haven't told anyone about the baby? It's because, even in these enlightened times, I know there's going to be a stigma attached to it because its mother isn't married. And because the fault is *mine*, I'm feeling guilty. And because Cassie and Naomi are on cloud nine over their babies, I didn't want to throw a shadow over *their* happiness.'

She came to rest on the far side of the room, suddenly running out of energy and feeling as if her legs had turned to over-cooked spaghetti, but there was still one point she hadn't covered.

'As for you,' she said softly, 'I'll never know why you didn't come to your senses years ago and marry and have a family of your own, but I'd *never* do anything to stop you seeing this little one if you wanted to. If I get the consultancy at St Augustine's, you might even find yourself co-opted into babysitting on a regular basis over the next dozen or so years, especially if it turns out to be as stubborn and bull-headed as its father,' she threatened, suddenly strangely light-headed.

By the time she ran out of words she was swaying on her feet and Sam's harsh curse seemed to come from a long way away as the walls receded into darkness and the floor started to come up to meet her.

The last thought Kirstin had was an impossible one—to wish that she had the courage to admit that she'd fallen in love with him. If Sam were to respond with a similar confession, she wouldn't care how many people found out about the baby. She'd even be willing to shout it from the rooftops...

'Stupid,' Sam was muttering over her as she opened her eyes and found herself lying on the settee. 'Stupid,' he repeated as she stared up into his face and saw the worry there that he wouldn't have shown to one of their patients.

'You or me?' she murmured, feeling a little out of it, almost as if she were drunk. He looked quite ominous, looming over her that way.

'Both, probably,' he said darkly, checking her pulse against his watch. 'When did you last eat?'

'Midday, of course…no. There was that emergency Caesarean that came in and then—'

'Kirstin.' He interrupted her meandering monologue sharply. 'Do you mean to tell me that you haven't eaten anything since that toast I made you this morning? No wonder you look as if you're fading away. You haven't got the sense God gave a goose.'

He straightened up and began to stride towards the door then stopped and turned to fix her with a piercing stare.

'You're to lie there until I come back,' he ordered. 'I'm going to get you something to eat.'

The scrambled eggs on toast Sam made were perfect and the ripe banana was just the way she liked them, but by the time he'd watched over her until she'd finished the large glass of milk he'd insisted on she was almost asleep where she sat.

'Bed,' Sam announced in his best don't-argue-with-me voice and she barely had enough energy to squeak when he swung her up into his arms, let alone dispute his orders.

She did object when he would have set off up the stairs with her in his arms.

'No,' Kirstin said stubbornly, holding onto the newel post at the bottom with a fresh surge of energy. 'I can walk and you can't afford to have a hernia. You wouldn't be able to operate for weeks while it healed and there are too many people who need your skill.'

He silently conceded the point but insisted on escorting her up the stairs with an arm protectively around her waist.

'Bathroom's all yours,' he said, leaving her at the open door.

She was about to close it behind her when her brain started functioning.

'Sam,' she called after him, and he whirled swiftly to face her as though expecting to see her collapsing again. 'It's just... I haven't got anything with me—clothing or toothbrush or...'

His shoulders relaxed again and he waved her back into the bathroom. 'I'll get you a clean T-shirt to wear and you'll find a new toothbrush in the cabinet.'

She was flagging again by the time she'd finished her cursory bedtime preparations, and was almost relieved to find Sam waiting outside the door to escort her to his bed.

She knew she should talk to him about the fact that she needed to get some clothes ready for the morning, but before she could speak he pressed the tips of his fingers to her lips.

'Sleep, Kirstin,' he ordered gently as he pulled the covers up to her chin. 'I'll take care of things. You just sleep.'

A little voice in the back of her head was trying to tell her that she ought to be objecting to his autocratic ways, but it was just so nice to feel cherished that she didn't bother to listen to it.

The bed was every bit as comfortable as she remembered and as she snuggled into the pillow she drew in the indefinable mixture of musk and soap and man that her body would always recognise as...

'Sam,' she whispered softly.

'Yes?' he answered immediately, much to her surprise. She'd thought he'd already left the room but when she opened her eyes just a crack she could see him standing a little way away, looking at her.

'Aren't you coming, too?' she asked sleepily, the words distorted by a yawn. 'The bed's too cold without you.'

Kirstin was feeling on top of the world when she began scrubbing up for the first case on the list.

She hadn't slept so well for a long time and for some unknown reason she hadn't been nearly as sick this morning. Perhaps she was coming to the end of it. After all, not every woman automatically suffered from morning sickness and very few had it for exactly the duration of the first trimester.

Whatever the reason, she'd woken up to the sight of Sam sitting on the edge of the bed still wrapped in his towelling dressing-gown while he presented her with a perfect piece of toast.

'Tea? Glucose drink?' he offered while she nibbled.

'Tea, please,' she asked, hoping fervently that the familiar feeling of nausea would wait until she'd had a chance to put something in her stomach.

She knew she would probably be all right until she tried to get out of bed, but she could hardly stay there when there was a full operating list to get through today. The fact that she was lying in *Sam's* bed was just another attraction, and the vague memories of being held safely in his arms all night could just as easily have been a memory of that first weekend.

In the end there had even been time for another

slice of toast before Sam took her home to shower and dress for the day ahead.

Neither of them had said anything about their discussion the previous evening. Kirstin had been too busy concentrating on the state of her stomach to be able to hold a rational conversation, and Sam had quietly gone about his own preparations for the day for all the world as if they'd shared a bathroom for years.

In spite of the fact that they kept verbal exchanges to a minimum, it was clear that something in the atmosphere surrounding them had changed.

There was a new ease between them, or perhaps it was a return of the empathy that had been developing before.

Whatever it was, it had put a spring in Kirstin's step and a smile on her face as she prepared for the full day ahead with a return of her old eagerness.

Eight hours later she was totally exhausted but well pleased with the way the day had gone.

Sam, too, had seemed satisfied, in spite of the extra pressure on him to supervise Kirstin's technique.

There had been several complicated cases including one patient who'd needed a hysterectomy and bladder repair, both of which had to be effected from below due to extensive scarring across her lower abdomen.

Sam had even gone so far as to joke that the patient would undoubtedly appreciate the fact that Kirstin's hands were smaller and more agile than his, but he'd been quite serious when he'd congratulated her on a neat job.

Of all the cases on the list, Sahru's had been the one she'd been most anxious about, and it was the first time Kirstin had really appreciated the difference it could make if she already knew a patient before they appeared as an operative case. She'd readily understood why Hal had declined to perform the anaesthetic for the woman he loved.

Sam had performed Sahru's operation himself and he'd been meticulous about explaining exactly what he'd been going to do.

He was utterly focused and professional, nevertheless Kirstin recognised a current of suppressed anger in his voice and she tried to remember when she had first started to become aware of his hidden emotions.

It was late by the time they were happy enough with all their post-operative patients to go home. In spite of the fact that it was a crisp dry evening Sam insisted on giving her a lift, but Kirstin was equally insistent on going to her own flat.

She would have loved to have spent another night wrapped in the safety of Sam's arms, but it would be far too dangerous to become accustomed to it. She had fought long and hard to secure her independence and she wasn't going to risk losing it now—she couldn't afford to if she was going to be able to take care of her baby.

It was still dark when the first pain ripped across Kirstin's stomach, but it was the insidious trickle between her legs that started with the second pain that had her reaching for the telephone.

'Sam,' she quavered, conscious of the panic in her high-pitched voice. It had taken her endless seconds to force her brain to remember his number.

'Kirstin?' His deep voice sounded hoarse and it was obvious that she'd woken him out of a sound sleep. 'What's the matter, Kirstin? Problem with one of the post-ops?'

'Sam, please…help me,' she said, then gasped as another pain sliced through her. She closed her eyes and fought for control when all she wanted to do was scream.

'Kirstin, what's wrong?' he demanded, fully awake now and concern clear in his voice even down a telephone line.

'Oh, Sam…' she wailed, the first devastated tears trickling down her face. 'I'm… I think I'm losing the baby.'

CHAPTER TEN

'GET the ultrasound equipment in here as quickly as possible. And she'll need an IV line. Ritodrine. Start her on fifty micrograms per minute and slowly increase it to two hundred and fifty,' Kirstin heard Sam snap, and she squeezed her eyes shut.

This was definitely one of those times when knowing too much was a bad thing.

To know that the drug he'd just ordered was the one they most often used to prevent premature labour brought home the reality of her situation as nothing else could have.

She'd been existing in something of a make-believe world over the last few months, convincing herself that if she wanted something badly enough, she would be able to make it happen.

In a strange way, the baby had never been more real than now when it seemed as if she was losing it.

The staff were well used to hiding their reactions, but when Sam had lifted her out of bed and had seen the amount of blood she'd lost, he hadn't been able to hide his response.

He hadn't said anything, but she'd known then that there was little hope that their child could survive.

'Oh, Sam, I'm sorry...' Kirstin whispered as the helpless tears slid from the corners of her eyes and into her hair.

Even with her eyes closed she knew when he came close, and when he threaded his fingers through hers she clung to him with a surge of gratitude. Even that sort of innocent connection was like balm to her spirit.

'When's the technician coming with the ultrasound?' Sam demanded impatiently, and she tightened her grip. Her heart felt as if it was trying to beat its way out of her chest and she was trembling all over, but she didn't think it was an adverse reaction to the drug now coursing through her veins.

'Kirstin, listen to me,' he whispered urgently when she whimpered, and she turned her head to find his face right beside her.

His eyes were filled with the searing intensity she remembered from that fateful forty-eight hours and had believed she'd never see again.

'Just remember, whatever happens, whether you've lost the baby or not, I'll be here for you,' he said insistently, his voice low enough for his words to be concealed by the bustle going on around them.

'If you want to try again,' he continued urgently, 'all you have to do is ask. I can't think of anyone I would rather have as the mother of my child.'

'Oh, Sam,' she breathed, more touched than she could say. How had he known what to say to take the sharpest edge off the agony of loss?

It didn't stop the misery of uncertainty as she waited for the trolley of ultrasound equipment to arrive.

It still seemed to take for ever before the pale blue lubricating jelly was squeezed into a heap midway between her hipbones and the probe positioned.

There was an almost unearthly silence as the technician tilted and slid the instrument in different directions, initially to spread the jelly and then to take a reading.

Knowing that there would be no curled-up tadpole-like figure to see, Kirstin couldn't bear to watch the screen where the shadowy images of her empty uterus would appear. She focused instead on the lean planes of Sam's face and tried to console herself with the fact that he was willing to go through all this again.

The prospect of weeks of miserable mornings while she went through another spell of morning sickness was well worth the memories she would have of an-other forty-eight hours of ecstasy.

First she would ask Sam to put her through what-ever tests he could think of to rule out the possibility of this happening again. She didn't think she could bear to lose another child. How did other women manage to stay sane when they lost three, four or even more?

'Kirstin?' Sam prompted, drawing her attention by cradling her cheek in one hand.

She was vaguely aware of the fascinated gaze of their colleagues at the unexpectedly tender gesture, but it was the expression in Sam's eyes that mattered.

The darkness of pain had gone. Instead, the deep brown almost seemed to gleam with sparks of gold.

'Look, Kirstin,' he urged with a shaky smile, turn-ing her towards the fateful screen. 'She's still there, sweetheart. Our baby's still there.'

There was a collective gasp at his revealing words but Kirstin didn't care any more. All she was inter-ested in was the image of the child nestled deep inside her.

'Can you see the heart beating, my love?' Sam said softly, his voice husky in the sudden silence as he used one long finger to point to the image. 'That started beating when she was just twenty days old and will continue until she's a very old lady. Her arms and legs are already moving but she's just too small for you to feel it yet.'

The sound of someone blowing their nose intruded on the oasis of delighted discovery and Kirstin glanced up into Cassie's tear-reddened eyes.

Naomi was just behind her... In fact, the whole room seemed to be full of friends and colleagues unashamedly wallowing in what seemed to be a happy ending.

'Oh, Sam, I'm sorry,' she wailed softly, turning her head into his shoulder. 'Now everybody knows.'

'And about time, too,' he growled as he speared his fingers through her hair and cradled her gently. 'Now perhaps we can stop tiptoeing around and get a few more things out into the open.'

'Only if they're things you don't mind the whole of St Augustine's knowing,' the medical technician warned as she packed her equipment away. 'You've probably already got the gossip piranhas in a feeding frenzy. By the way,' she added and held out a piece of paper, 'here's the first picture for the album.'

Sam held it up so that Kirstin could see the shadowy images printed in black and white.

'Do you really think it's a girl?' she asked, feeling her smile tremble on her lips.

'A little girl with her mother's beautiful hair and mesmerising eyes,' he said firmly. 'And if it isn't, we'll have to have another try until we get it right.'

There was a new determination in his voice which Kirstin hadn't heard before, and it was evident in the expression in his eyes, too.

'Kirstin, you know about my problem so you know I'm no great catch, but would you please put me out of my misery and marry me?'

'What?' she gasped, the sound almost completely lost in the sudden cheer that Naomi and Cassie let out.

She glanced around the stark room, filled with an assortment of equipment which she'd spent years learning about and felt a growing panic.

This wasn't supposed to happen. She had been very careful not to get too close to anyone to make *certain* that it didn't. She'd concentrated on her career to make sure that she never had to depend on other people for her happiness.

It was rooms like these, in a hospital like St Augustine's, that were going to provide the stability in her life so that she could support her child.

Hospitals didn't die and leave you all alone in the world. Hospitals didn't reject you because you weren't pretty enough to adopt or…

'But, Sam, you know I can't,' she quavered as a new pain began to grow inside her, this one centred around her heart. 'I told you right from the start that I would never let myself be dependent on anyone.'

'I'm not asking you to, Kirstin,' Sam retorted softly, brushing a stray tear away with gentle knuckles. 'What I'm asking is if you'll let *me* depend on *you*.'

'Depend on me?' she said in confusion, marginally aware that the room was suddenly very empty. 'But—'

'Our baby is depending on you at the moment for her very existence,' he continued in a soothing voice. 'But once she's born she'll gradually grow in independence until she can stand on her own two feet in the world.'

He paused a moment and cradled her cheek with his other hand, tilting her face to make certain she was giving him all her attention.

'That won't happen to me,' he declared, and brushed a tender kiss over her lips that left them tingling. 'It couldn't, because I love you and I'll never stop needing you, in my life, in my home, in my arms.'

His lips met hers again and she was powerless to stop herself responding. It had been that way between them right from the first time, if only she'd been honest enough to admit it, and she couldn't imagine what her life would be like without Sam in it.

'But—' Her determination to cope with things on her own was too well ingrained not to make her object. She didn't get very far.

'In the end,' he interrupted, 'it all comes down to those three little words. I love you, Kirstin. I've loved you ever since you joined the department and I've been slowly going out of my mind, waiting for you to fall for some young handsome doctor who would sweep you off your feet and out of my life. It was a dream come true when you propositioned me—'

'I did not!' she exclaimed heatedly. 'I just came to ask you to let me have DI. If you hadn't tried so hard to talk me out of it, I'd never have got so hot under the collar and I'd never have had the courage to ask you.'

'Well, you've put me through hell, woman,' he complained, settling her into a more comfortable position, although when she'd ended up cradled across his lap she didn't know. 'All you wanted was a donation from me when I wanted you to want the donor as well.'

He smoothed the tangled strands away from her cheeks then buried his hand in them again to cradle her head against his shoulder.

Kirstin could hear the steady, powerful beat of his heart through the wall of his chest and thought of that other tiny heart fluttering deep inside her.

She had so many things to be grateful for. She would owe Sam her thanks for ever for all the things he'd done for her. He'd been utterly steadfast in supporting her even when there had been little more than a tentative friendship between them.

Even when their alliance seemed to have completely broken down he hadn't abandoned her...but, then, he was Sam, and Sam wasn't like that.

'You didn't answer,' he reminded her in a husky voice, and for the first time since he'd seen the proof that their tiny baby was still alive she could feel the tension in him.

'Answer? What was the question?' So much had happened in the last couple of hours and it still felt like the middle of the night so her brain wasn't responding very fast.

Sam groaned theatrically and slid her off his lap and back onto the bed.

Kirstin wasn't sure what to make of his abandonment until she caught sight of the gleam in his eyes.

'I suppose you want me to do this in the properly approved manner,' he grumbled as he went down on one knee on the hospital floor. 'Kirstin Whittaker, I love you completely, utterly, permanently, and I need you in my life to make it worth living. Will you do me the honour of marrying me, even if it's only to take pity on my ruined reputation?'

Kirstin found herself chuckling through her tears and realised suddenly that Sam was the only man who would ever be able to make her laugh and cry at the same time. It was all so obvious in the end. He wouldn't have been able to affect her so much if she hadn't loved him all along.

'As you're the only man who ever tempted me into propositioning him, I suppose we'd better get married,' she said with a tentative smile. 'But the most important reason will always be those three little words. I love you,' she declared softly, and her heart melted when she saw the sheen of tears brighten his eyes, too.

'I've got a surprise for you, Kirstin,' Sam announced over the hubbub of the joint party Cassie, Naomi and Kirstin had thrown for the christenings of their babies.

The poor clergyman had been completely muddled by the fact that each couple had chosen the other two to stand as godparents to their own child.

'But it keeps it all in the family,' Cassie had declared with simple logic. 'If anything ever happened to any of us, we would automatically look after each other's children anyway. This will just make it official.'

Dot was in seventh heaven, her arms apparently permanently full of one baby or the other so that Kirstin was beginning to wonder whether she'd put a special spell on them so that they would wake up one at a time.

Sam took her hand and began to tow her across the room, and she suddenly remembered what he'd said.

'A surprise? You mean, like finding out that it really *was* a daughter I was carrying?' she teased. They'd both adamantly refused to find out in advance of the delivery, and Kirstin had been able to tell from the expression on Sam's face that he'd actually been as surprised as she'd been when the baby arrived.

There had been times when she'd been seriously tempted to cheat, but in the end it had been enough just to know that the baby had existed and had been growing strong and healthy.

'That wasn't just a surprise but a delight,' he corrected her. 'Especially when you decided you wouldn't limit me to the one just because I'd got what I wanted the first time.'

Kirstin gave him a dig in the ribs, still amazed at the changes marriage and fatherhood had made to the serious, work-driven man she used to know. His face seemed almost permanently wreathed in smiles these days, and never more so than when he was holding their daughter.

'As I was saying,' he continued, 'we might have got the conception and the marriage slightly in the wrong order, but when we applied for the licence I happened to notice something on your birth certificate.'

He pulled the official document out of the inside pocket of his jacket, answering her unasked question about why he was still wearing it so long after they'd returned from the church.

'You've probably never had cause to study it before, but I noticed that there were some figures in the column for the date of birth.'

They had reached the relative peace of the hallway by then and he unfolded it and handed it to her.

'As you probably know, the only reason why a specific time of birth is recorded is in the case of multiple births, to distinguish which sibling was born first.'

Kirstin was gazing at the evidence in disbelief. It was taking more than a few seconds to sink in.

'You mean, there was more than one of me?' she demanded in amazement.

'Not exactly,' he corrected with a chuckle. 'But there were two of you born that day, and knowing that, and the fact that you've always felt the lack of any blood relative, I started to make a few enquiries.'

'And you found her?' she demanded excitedly, not certain whether she wanted to fling her arms around him or dance in circles. 'Oh, Sam, tell me you found my twin!'

'Yes, I found your twin,' he agreed as he reached for the door to the room they'd finally decorated as a dining room and swung it open. 'But she's a he,' he finished.

Kirstin stood in the doorway and gazed in disbelief at the little group of people waiting to meet her.

The man was taller than she was and his shoulders were broader, but the similarities in their facial features and colouring were almost uncanny.

'Hello, Kirstin, I'm Christopher,' he said as he ushered the woman and child beside him forward to meet her. 'And this is Penny, my wife, and our daughter, Kirstin, who was born three weeks and one day ago.'

'The same day,' Kirstin whispered as the uncanny coincidence raised all the hairs on the back of her neck. 'Sam, did you hear that? We had our babies on the same day.'

Sam must have felt her every quiver because he

tightened his arm around her shoulders in a silent gesture of support.

'And we'd already named her Kirstin before Sam tracked us down,' Penny said with a tearful smile. 'I wanted to give her my mother's name but Christopher was adamant that her name was Kirstin.'

A sudden burst of laughter reminded Kirstin that they had a houseful of guests. Torn between her duties as hostess and her need to spend time with the brother she'd never known existed, she sent a desperate look in Sam's direction.

'I've invited them to stay for a few days—if you've no objections,' he teased. 'But I do think you ought to warn them about the mad mob they're about to become part of in case they want to change their minds and make a quick exit.'

'It's a joint christening party,' she explained. 'There were three of us in my last foster-home and we became the family we'd lost. Now we've all had children and the family has grown.'

Christopher turned a loving smile on Penny. 'We met in a foster-home, too, and are busy creating a family of our own. Don't you think it'll grow much quicker if we join forces?' He had a slightly diffident expression on his face as he held his hand out, but Kirstin answered the invitation by flinging herself into his arms.

'Oh, Sam, just wait till Dot finds out about this,' she exclaimed tearfully. 'She'll have another baby to spoil.'

'Oh, Sam, what a perfect day!' Kirstin said in a careful whisper, very aware of the sleeping infant in the cot beside the bed. And just on the other side of the hallway there was another child lying in another cot.

'Today it was almost like being in one of those carnival sideshows where everywhere you look there are mirrors,' she said with a watery giggle. 'Everywhere there were couples with little babies.'

'Can you imagine what it's going to be like each Christmas? And what about all the birthday parties?' Sam demanded.

'And then there are all the other babies to invite as they arrive,' Kirstin pointed out. 'Did you know that Sahru's pregnant already? She and Hal only got married six weeks ago.'

'Slow workers,' Sam said dismissively. 'I know a couple who managed it in forty-eight hours.'

'Sam!' She aimed a smack at him but he captured her hand and planted a loving kiss in her palm.

'How do you fancy seeing if we can break our record when we're ready for another one?' he suggested wickedly, and her heartbeat instantly began to speed up.

'Oh, yes, please,' she whispered, and slid her hand up over his chest to cradle his jaw.

He wrapped her in his arms and life became perfect. She knew she was never going to regret the day they'd finally found the courage to exchange those three little words.

MILLS & BOON®

Makes any time special™

Mills & Boon publish 29 new titles every month. Select from...

Modern Romance™   Tender Romance™

Sensual Romance™

Medical Romance™   Historical Romance™

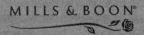

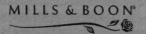

0102/98/MB10
MILLS & BOON
THIS TIME...
MARRIAGE
Three brides get the chance to make it This Time... Forever.
Great value—
3 compelling novels in 1.
Available from 2nd February 2001

4 FREE
books and a surprise gift!

We would like to take this opportunity to thank you for reading this Mills & Boon® book by offering you the chance to take FOUR more specially selected titles from the Medical Romance™ series absolutely FREE! We're also making this offer to introduce you to the benefits of the Reader Service™—

★ FREE home delivery
★ FREE gifts and competitions
★ FREE monthly Newsletter
★ Exclusive Reader Service discounts
★ Books available before they're in the shops

Accepting these FREE books and gift places you under no obligation to buy, you may cancel at any time, even after receiving your free shipment. Simply complete your details below and return the entire page to the address below. *You don't even need a stamp!*

YES! Please send me 4 free Medical Romance books and a surprise gift. I understand that unless you hear from me, I will receive 6 superb new titles every month for just £2.40 each, postage and packing free. I am under no obligation to purchase any books and may cancel my subscription at any time. The free books and gift will be mine to keep in any case.

M1ZEA

Ms/Mrs/Miss/Mr ....Initials................................
BLOCK CAPITALS PLEASE

Surname ....

Address ....

....

....Postcode................................

Send this whole page to:
UK: FREEPOST CN81, Croydon, CR9 3WZ
EIRE: PO Box 4546, Kilcock, County Kildare (stamp required)